THE BOBBSEY TWINS
MYSTERY AT MEADOWBROOK

At that moment Rocket shied violently

The Bobbsey Twins' Mystery at Meadowbrook

By

LAURA LEE HOPE

GROSSET & DUNLAP

Publishers • New York

Published in 2004 by Grosset & Dunlap, a division of Penguin Young
Readers Group, 345 Hudson Street, New York, New York 10014.
GROSSET & DUNLAP is a trademark of Penguin Group (USA) Inc.
THE BOBBSEY TWINS® is a registered trademark of
Simon & Schuster, Inc.

Printed in the U.S.A.

ISBN 0-448-43758-9

3 5 7 9 10 8 6 4 2

CONTENTS

"Where is Harry?" asked Flossie

CHAPTER I

A FURRY PASSENGER

"WHERE is Harry?" asked Flossie Bobbsey, as she jumped down from the train steps and looked around the deserted station platform. "He was supposed to meet us."

"And Uncle Daniel too," said her blond, blue-eyed twin brother Freddie, who was in back of her.

Freddie and Flossie, six years old, were followed by the older Bobbsey twins, dark-haired Bert and Nan, who were twelve. Each carried a suitcase.

Behind the children came a jolly-looking woman who puffed as she eased herself down the steep steps. She was Dinah Johnson, who had lived with the Bobbsey family as long as the twins could remember. She helped Mrs. Bobbsey with the housework.

"Flossie," Dinah called, "here's your pocketbook. You left it on the seat in the train!"

"Oh, thank you, Dinah!" The little girl ran up and took the white leather bag. "I wouldn't lose it for anything. It's my very favorite!"

"I wonder why Uncle Daniel isn't here," Nan said worriedly.

"I s'pect they'll be along in a minute," Dinah said, fanning herself. This was a hot summer day. "It takes a while to drive in from Meadowbrook Farm. They know we're coming to visit, so they'll be here."

"I can hardly wait to see Cousin Harry," said Bert. "He and I always have a good time together."

"And I want to see Aunt Sarah and Martha," Nan added. Martha lived at the farm with the Daniel Bobbseys.

By this time the visitors' suitcases and boxes had been placed side by side at the edge of the platform. There still was no sign of the Meadowbrook Bobbseys.

"Freddie," Dinah cautioned, "you take care of Snoop. Be sure he don't go gallivantin' out of that case!"

Snoop was the black cat whom Freddie had been given after he had been locked in a big department store by mistake.

The little boy giggled as he crouched down

and peered through the wire window of the carrying case. "Snoop looks like a tiger in a cage!" he observed. "He'll be glad when we get him to the farm, and he can chase mice in the barn."

"I wish Snap had come with us," Flossie said. She meant the shaggy white dog who had adopted the Bobbsey family during the MYS-TERY AT SCHOOL.

"He'll have a good time with Sam, Dinah," Nan spoke up. "He can ride around on Dad's lumber truck with Sam, and you know how he likes that."

"You're right," Flossie agreed. "And when Mommy and Daddy come home from the lumber invention, he'll have even more people to ride around with!"

"*Con*vention, Flossie," Nan corrected her sister with a smile.

Bert had been watching two men lift a small crate from the baggage car. Now he exclaimed, "There's something alive in there! I saw it move!"

"Where?" Flossie wanted to know, straightening up and following Bert's glance.

"Let's go look!" Freddie urged, and started to run down the platform. The other children followed.

By the time they arrived, the crate stood on a

baggage truck. The men had returned to the train, which pulled slowly out of the station.

Flossie stood on tiptoes and peeked between the slats of the box. "Ooh!" she exclaimed. "It's a baby bear!"

"Let me see!" Freddie cried excitedly.

While the small twins peered at the crated animal, Bert examined the tag. "It's addressed to Mr. T. E. Holden," he reported.

"Holden!" Nan exclaimed. "Do you suppose he's Tom Holden's father? You know, we met Tom and his little brother Roy the last time we visited at Meadowbrook. He's a friend of Harry's."

"Could be," Bert replied. "But why would Tom's father be getting a bear cub?"

"Maybe it's a pet," Freddie suggested. "I'd like to have a little bear at our house!"

"It would be scary though, when it got bigger!" Flossie said.

Nan looked around. "I don't understand why Uncle Daniel isn't here," she said, puzzled. "Do you think anything has happened to him?"

The children walked slowly back to Dinah. "Maybe you'd better telephone out to the farm, Nan," Dinah said. "Your uncle may have thought we were coming tomorrow."

Nan ran into the station to make the call. In a few minutes, she was back. "Aunt Sarah says Uncle Daniel and Harry left the farm almost an hour ago," she reported.

"Here they come!" Freddie shouted as an open farm truck drew up to the station. A blond, athletic-looking boy of Bert's age jumped out. He was followed by a tall, dark-haired man.

After they had all greeted one another, Uncle Daniel said apologetically, "Sorry you have to ride in the truck, and it's too bad we kept you waiting. We stopped at the Holdens' farm and stayed longer than we had expected." He glanced toward the baggage cart. "That must be the crate Mr. Holden asked us to pick up."

"We know what's in it!" Flossie said, her blue eyes shining with mischief. "A baby bear!"

Uncle Daniel rumpled his niece's curls. "You don't say!" he exclaimed. "Still playing detective, are you?"

The Bobbsey twins loved to solve mysteries, and something exciting always seemed to happen wherever they went.

"Why is Mr. Holden getting a bear?" Freddie asked curiously.

"Tom and his father are running an animal farm now," Harry replied. He explained that the Holdens had a collection of animals common to that area.

"Tourists driving by stop and pay to see them," Harry went on. He grinned. "It's a good business."

"Say, that sounds terrific!" Bert remarked. "I'd like to see the animals some time."

"You can when we deliver the bear," Harry said.

"But what about the bear?" Nan spoke up. "He certainly didn't come from *this* area, did he?"

Harry shook his head. "No, I don't think there are any bears around here now." Then he told the twins that as a sideline Mr. Holden was training a few bear cubs.

"When they're as young as this one, they're quite tame and easy to teach. Then Mr. Holden sells them to circuses and carnivals."

While the children were talking, Uncle Daniel had gone into the station to sign a receipt for the crate. In a few minutes, he came out.

"All right, everybody," he said jovially. "Who wants to put the bear in the truck?"

"I do!" Freddie volunteered eagerly, jumping up and raising his arm high.

Uncle Daniel laughed. "I think you'd find him a little heavy, Freddie! You'd better let Harry and Bert do it."

The little bear did prove to be extremely heavy for his size. The two boys staggered under the weight of the crate as they carried it the short distance between the baggage cart and the truck. Uncle Daniel and Dinah had already put the luggage and Snoop in his carrying case into the back of the truck.

"May Freddie and I ride with the bear?" Flossie asked, jumping up and down in excitement.

"Let's all ride back there," Bert proposed. Dinah grinned broadly. "You can excuse me," she said firmly. "I don't aim to ride with a bear —even if he is a baby!"

"You can sit up front with me, Dinah," Uncle Daniel said with a twinkle in his eyes. "I'm not fond of bears either!"

Nan decided she would sit with Dinah and Uncle Daniel, but the others all climbed into the body of the truck. With much squirming and laughing, they settled themselves on the floor between the cab and the bear crate.

"Take it easy, Dad!" Harry called as his father drove away from the station. "Remember we haven't any cushions back here!"

Flossie was nearest the crate. She stuck her face close to the slats. "Hello, bear," she said. "We're going for a ride."

"Be careful, Flossie," Harry warned. "Some of those slats have worked loose. He might be able to get his paw out and scratch you."

"I don't think he'd hurt me!" Flossie protested. "He likes me!"

"He wouldn't mean to," Harry explained, "but bears can't pull in their claws the way cats can."

"Snoop wouldn't scratch anyone!" Freddie said proudly.

"Of course not!" Flossie agreed.

Hearing his name, the cat meowed loudly. At once the bear gave a low growl.

"Oh!" cried Flossie, and pulled over against Bert.

As the truck rumbled on toward the Bobbsey farm, Harry told the others more things he had learned about bears since the Holdens had opened their animal exhibit.

"They have five toes on all four feet," he said. "Cats and dogs have only four toes on their back feet."

"Let's count Snoop's toes," Freddie suggested, starting to open the carrying case.

"You'd better not do that," Bert warned. "Snoop might want to get away from the bear and jump off the truck."

"And he might run away forever!" Flossie cried out.

"Okay," Freddie agreed cheerfully. "I'll wait until we get to the farm. Tell us some more about bears, Harry!"

"They love to climb trees," his cousin said, "and they're pretty good at it. Mr. Holden says most bears can swim too!"

"I wonder if they can dive," Flossie giggled.

"Flossie! Your purse!" Harry exclaimed.

The little girl looked bewildered. "What's the matter?" Then she glanced at the floor of the truck where she had laid her precious white handbag.

She saw that the bear had managed to get one paw out of the crate and had hooked his claws around the handle of the bag.

"Give that back to me, you naughty bear!" Flossie ordered sternly as the cub drew the purse toward him. She put out her hand to grab the bag.

"I'll get it for you, Flossie!" Bert cried. He struggled to his feet and made his way toward the crate.

But just as he reached it, the truck hit a hole in the road. The bump threw Bert off balance, and he skidded into the wooden box. The jolt unfastened the tail gate. An instant later the crate fell from the truck with a *crash!*

"Oh! Oh!" Flossie screamed. "The bear will be hurt!"

As the box hit the road, the slats on one side splintered. Out rolled the bear! He scrambled to his stumpy little legs and loped off!

CHAPTER II

SCARED RABBITS

"CATCH HIM! Catch him!" Flossie screamed as the furry little animal waddled across the road and slid into a ditch.

At the sound of the commotion behind him, Uncle Daniel pulled the truck to the side of the road and stopped.

Nan looked back. "It's the bear!" she cried. "He's loose!"

Quickly Uncle Daniel jumped down, followed by Nan. Flossie and the three boys had scrambled from the back of the truck as soon as it stopped. In the middle of the road lay Flossie's bag. She stooped to pick it up.

By this time the bear had crossed the ditch to a field and was calmly tearing blueberries from a clump of bushes with his long snout.

"Bring me the rope from the truck, Harry!" Uncle Daniel instructed. "I'll try to lasso the little fellow."

10

Harry ran for the coil and put it into his father's hand. The farmer cautiously approached the bear, a loop of rope ready to be tossed over the animal's head.

Freddie followed closely. Then suddenly he cried, "Look! The bear's wearing a collar!"

The leather collar had a metal name plate on it, which gleamed in the sunlight.

The cub continued to eat unconcernedly. He paid no attention as Uncle Daniel slipped one end of the rope under the collar and tied it.

"He's really tame!" Bert commented.

Nan had read the lettering on the collar. "His name is Arthur!" she announced.

Flossie giggled. "That's a funny name for a bear!"

"Come on, Arthur!" said Harry, as he took the rope from his father and pulled the animal away from the bushes.

Arthur did not want to leave his meal of berries and planted his four feet firmly on the ground. Bert went to Harry's assistance. Together the two boys dragged the reluctant bear toward the road.

Finally, the little animal gave up and ambled back to the truck. The boys lifted him inside, and Harry tied the rope to a side post. With a grunt, Arthur lay down, put his head on his paws, and went to sleep.

Nan climbed into the rear with the other children, and Uncle Daniel started the truck. Dinah settled back with a sigh of relief.

"If I'd had some honey along," she said, "I'd sure have caught him easy."

Flossie sat down as far away from the bear as she could. "He might wake up and want my pocketbook again!" she explained seriously, clutching the white bag to her.

Nan laughed. "There's always something exciting happening at Meadowbrook!" she observed.

Harry snapped his fingers. "That reminds me—I forgot to tell you about our mystery!"

"A mystery!" the twins chorused. "What is it?"

Their cousin told them that there had been a series of bank robberies in several small towns nearby. "The robbers always get away," he concluded. "The police haven't been able to catch them!"

"Ooh! I hope they don't come around here!" Flossie exclaimed.

"We'll catch them if they do!" Freddie spoke up bravely.

"Dad's on the board of directors of the Meadowbrook Bank," Harry went on. "He and the others are afraid the robbers will come there some time."

Before any more could be said about the bank robberies, the truck turned into a lane. It led to the Daniel Bobbseys' comfortable-looking, white farmhouse.

"Here we are!" Uncle Daniel called out. When he stopped at the side of the house, a door flew open and Aunt Sarah and Martha, the cook, hurried outside.

Aunt Sarah was short and plump and had a merry smile. Martha was tall and thin and had twinkling blue eyes.

While Aunt Sarah threw her arms around the twins and kissed them, Martha welcomed Dinah and walked around to help her take some of the smaller luggage from the truck.

"Good gracious!" she exclaimed when she saw the little bear tied to the post. "What have you got here?"

"That's Arthur," Harry explained. "He belongs to Mr. Holden. We're going to take him over there in a little while."

"Well, I hope so!" Martha said briskly. "We have enough pets around here. We don't need a bear!"

Bert joined them and helped Harry with the larger suitcases. "By the way," he said, "how's our old pal, Rocket?"

"He's fine!" Harry assured him. "Do you want to go out to the barn and see him?"

Aunt Sarah threw her arms around the twins

Rocket was the little brown-and-white Shetland pony which the twins' mother had bought for them at an auction in Meadowbrook on a previous visit to the farm.

"Take your things up to your rooms first," Aunt Sarah suggested. "And you might as well change into your country clothes."

In a few minutes the children were downstairs again, dressed in shirts and blue jeans.

"Now you look more like farmers!" Uncle Daniel said when they came out to the barn.

"There's Rocket!" Nan cried happily, running up to the stall where the pony stood with his head resting on the top bar of the gate.

Flossie stroked him while Rocket rubbed his velvety nose against Nan's shoulder.

After Freddie and Bert also had greeted the pony, Uncle Daniel called to them, "Ready to go to the Holdens' now? We have a couple of hours before supper."

"Oh, yes," they answered, and scrambled into the truck again. Arthur sat on his haunches and peered around nearsightedly. It was a short ride to the Holden place. Harry pointed out the animal farm as they turned into the drive.

Under the trees to the right of the lane were a number of wire cages. In most of them, the twins could see an animal restlessly pacing back and forth.

"I guess they don't like being penned up," Nan thought.

Tom Holden sat behind a little table which bore a printed sign:

Holden's Animal Farm. Admission 25¢

When the truck stopped, the tall, dark-haired boy jumped up and ran over to it. "Hi, there!" he called. "It's great to see you twins again!"

Greetings were exchanged, then Bert and Harry lifted the little bear from the truck. "Here's Arthur!" Harry announced with a grin.

"He's a cute little fellow," Tom said admiringly. "Thanks for bringing him. We'll put Arthur in with the other cubs."

He led the way toward a piece of ground surrounded by a high wire fence. Inside the enclosure were four bear cubs about the same size as Arthur.

"Ooh, look!" Flossie exclaimed in delight. "They're dancing!"

A record player stood just outside the fence. To the strains of a waltz, two cubs were moving about on their hind legs.

"Dad taught them to do that," Tom explained proudly. "Here he comes now."

A tall, ruddy-faced man turned off the record and came toward them.

"Welcome to our animal farm!" Mr. Holden said. "Would you like to look around?"

The children nodded eagerly and followed their host over to another enclosure. As they entered it, two dainty, reddish-brown animals with white spots walked up to them.

"These are baby deer, or fawns," Mr. Holden remarked. "They're only about three months old. They'll keep their white spots for four or five months."

He handed pieces of apple to Freddie and Flossie. "Would you like to feed them?"

Flossie held the fruit on the palm of her hand and stretched it out to one of the fawns. "Ooh, he tickles!" She giggled as the baby deer took the apple with its soft lips.

When Freddie had given his apple to the other deer, the group moved on to several small cages. In the first one was another reddish-colored animal. This one had pointed ears and a bushy tail.

"This is a red fox," Mr. Holden explained. "We caught him here in our woods."

As the children watched, the fox walked up and down, eyeing the visitors with distrust. The next cage held an animal with brownish fur and a tail with black rings around it. Across his face was a stripe of black which made the animal look as if he were wearing a mask.

"That's a raccoon!" Freddie cried. "I saw one once when Bert and I went camping!"

"You're right!" Mr. Holden said. "This fellow is one of our most amusing pets. He's very curious and mischievous."

Tom pointed to a muddy spot in the enclosure. "See the print he makes?" he asked.

"It looks just like a human being's!" Nan exclaimed in surprise.

"That's because he walks on the flat of his feet," Harry spoke up. "He shows all his five toes."

"And here are the rabbits," Tom remarked as the Bobbseys came to another pen. He pointed to a corner. A mother and father rabbit and their four babies sat in a nest of straw. They were nibbling on lettuce leaves.

"Oh, they're darling!" Flossie cried, crouching down to watch the little animals. "Look at their twitchy noses."

"That's all we have at our animal farm so far," Mr. Holden said, "but we hope to receive more animals."

"Come see my homing pigeons," Tom suggested. "Harry had so much fun with his, that I decided to get some too." He led the way toward the barn. Mr. Holden and Uncle Daniel walked back to the farmhouse.

Harry and the twins followed Tom, but when they passed the bear cage again, Flossie took Freddie's hand. "Let's watch them some more."

The cubs were chasing one another around the enclosure. Every once in a while, two of them would stand up on their hind legs and appear to be boxing.

Flossie giggled. "Aren't they funny?" she remarked.

At that moment a tall, dark-haired boy about Bert's age strolled into the yard. "That's Mark Teron!" Freddie whispered to his twin. "We saw him when we were at Meadowbrook the last time, remember? He was always teasing us!"

"I remember all right," said Flossie.

Freddie had been watching Mark, who had gone into the rabbit pen. Now the little boy ran over to join him. "What are you doing?" Freddie asked.

Mark jumped at the sound of Freddie's voice and turned around. "So you're here again!" he said. "I heard you were coming to visit Harry."

"What are you doing with the rabbits?" Freddie insisted.

"Nothing. I'm just looking at them. Any law against it?"

The mother rabbit was cuddling her babies. When Mark stooped down and picked up two of them, she and the father hopped about nervously.

"I don't think you're supposed to touch the baby bunnies," Freddie objected, stepping up

to the older boy. "You're scaring the mother
and father rabbit!"

"Oh, mind your own business!" Mark said
roughly. As he spoke, he gave Freddie a hard
shove which sent him staggering against the
wire fence.

"Stop that!" Flossie screamed. "He didn't
hurt you!"

Bert had come back to see what had happened to the small twins. When he heard Flossie cry out, he ran to the rabbit pen.

"Let my little brother alone!" he called to
Mark.

The bully dropped the rabbits and swung
around. "You make me!" he challenged.

Bert set his jaw and took a quick step toward
Mark.

CHAPTER III

THE CHASE

MARK tried to step back to avoid Bert's fist, but his foot slipped and he fell. Quickly Bert sat on him.

"Let me up!" Mark sputtered, trying to rise.

"Not until you promise to stop picking on kids smaller than you!" Bert replied grimly.

Mark managed to free his arms and grabbed Bert around the neck. At that moment Mr. Holden and Uncle Daniel came from the house. When they saw the two boys struggling on the ground, Mr. Holden ran up.

"Stop this fighting!" he ordered.

"Mark was bothering the rabbits!" Flossie protested as Bert stood up.

"I've told you before to stay away from the animals, Mark," Mr. Holden said sternly. "If you can't do that, don't come around here!"

Mark scrambled to his feet. "It wasn't my

fault," he grumbled. "Bert jumped on me!" Then with a glare, he stalked off.

Mr. Holden turned to Uncle Daniel. "I'd like you to take a look at the west field, if you have time." The two men walked off together.

"Come see Tom's pigeons," Bert said to the small twins. They made their way toward the barnyard.

Flossie looked up at the flat roof of the barn annex. On top was a strange-looking wooden structure, and next to it a space enclosed with wire netting.

"That's the pigeon loft," Bert explained. "The perches for the birds are inside the wooden part. The pigeons stay in the wire cage during the day to get the sunlight."

"How do we get up there?" Freddie asked.

"I'll show you." Bert led the way through the barn and up a stairway to the second story. There the windows reached to the floor. It was easy to step through one onto the flat roof of the extension.

Bert and the small twins found Nan and Harry in the loft with Tom. He was showing them the bands on the legs of twenty or thirty pigeons.

He picked up one of the tiny aluminum bands. "This is put around a bird's leg when it is just a week old," Tom explained. "At that age the hind toe can still be bent backwards so the ring can be slipped over the foot."

"What are those markings on the bands?" Nan asked curiously.

"Those are the registration numbers," Tom replied. "Harry's and my pigeons are registered with the Meadowbrook Pigeon Club."

"Do your pigeons fly home with messages when you let them loose out in the country?" Freddie queried.

Tom laughed. "They're trained to return to the loft from *anywhere!*" he said.

"What makes them come back?" Nan asked.

"They want to rejoin their mates and also get food and water." Tom explained that in pigeon races, one of a pair is entered in the race while the other stays in the nest. Then, the next time, they are switched. Wanting to be with its mate helps to bring the other bird home.

"See this trap?" Tom asked, pointing to a small opening in the side of the loft. "It's fixed so the bird can get into the loft but not out of it. He lands on that little board out there and then pushes open the trap door."

A pigeon flew to Tom's shoulder and leaned forward to peck at some seed the boy held in his hand.

"We don't feed the birds that stay in the loft

until just before the racers are due back. Then the racing pigeons hear the noise of the feeding and hurry to get into the loft."

"There's a lot more to training pigeons than I ever thought," Bert remarked.

"It's fun though," Harry said. "Tom and I are going to enter some of our pigeons in the race the Meadowbrook Club is having. We'll need one person to stay by the loft while someone else takes the birds out to start them on their flight. Do you want to help me?"

"Sure!" Bert agreed eagerly.

"And I'll help Tom!" Nan volunteered.

While Tom was showing the others the drinking fountains, bath pans, and food dishes for the birds, Flossie wandered out onto the roof again. She circled the wire enclosure watching the pigeons strutting about on the floor.

Suddenly one of the pigeons, with a whir of wings, landed on the wire in front of her. Flossie stepped back, startled. The next instant her feet slipped over the edge of the roof!

Frantically the little girl clawed the air until her fingers closed over a metal trough which ran around the side of the annex roof. She hung there helplessly swinging in the air.

"Help!" she screamed.

At the sound Bert and Nan ran from the loft followed by the others. Tom dashed through

Try as they might, they could not raise Flossie

the window into the barn. Bert and Nan threw themselves flat on the roof, and each grasped one of Flossie's wrists.

"Hold on, Flossie!" Nan directed. "We'll haul you up!"

But try as they might, they could not raise the little girl. It was all they could do to hold her without slipping off themselves.

"Freddie," Bert panted, "run and get Uncle Daniel!"

Just as Freddie turned to go back into the barn, they saw the top of a ladder settle against the edge of the roof. The next moment Tom's head appeared. He grasped Flossie firmly and set her feet on the rungs of the ladder.

Flossie held tightly to the sides of the ladder without moving. Nan reached forward to help, and saw a large tear roll down the little girl's cheek.

"It's okay, honey," she said, taking her hands. "You're safe now."

"I—I was awful scared," Flossie said, finally stepping onto the roof ahead of Tom. She clung to her sister for a moment.

Bert patted Flossie's blond head. "You were lucky this time—you can't fly the way a pigeon can!" he said cheerfully.

Flossie giggled and wiped her eyes. "Thank you for saving me, Tom," she said.

"It was quick thinking," Nan told him.

"Say, maybe you'd be good at catching the bank robbers!" Harry said as they all started back through the barn.

"I don't know what I'd do if I saw them," Tom confessed.

"I know what I'd do!" Freddie spoke up.

"What?" Bert asked him, playfully rumpling the little boy's hair.

"I'd grab them and yell 'HELP!'" Freddie boasted, turning red in the face.

"I'd help you hold them!" Flossie promised.

"I can hold them by myself," Freddie protested. "You can run for the policeman!"

Everyone laughed.

"What would *you* do if you met the robbers, Nan?" Tom wanted to know.

Nan thought a moment, then said, "I think I'd pretend I didn't see them, but I'd hurry off and telephone the police to come right away!"

The older boys were sure they could capture the robbers without any help from the police. "We'd take them straight to jail!" Bert assured the others with a grin.

When the twins and their friends came from the barn, they saw Uncle Daniel behind the wheel of the truck. "Come on, children!" he called. "They'll be expecting us at Meadowbrook in time for supper."

After many good-bys to Tom and his father, the five children climbed into the truck, and Uncle Daniel drove toward his farm.

When they reached it, Bert and Freddie went with Harry to do the evening chores. Nan and Flossie hurried into the house.

"Ooh! That looks good!" Flossie exclaimed as she watched Martha lift a bubbling casserole from the oven.

"Run and wash your hands," Dinah advised. "Supper's just about ready!"

A short time later, the Bobbseys seated themselves at the supper table. The conversation turned again to the subject of homing pigeons.

"I've been taking a couple of birds out every day," Harry said. "I let them loose, and they fly back to my loft. I've lost two or three birds who couldn't find their way home, but that's a pretty good record."

"How far can pigeons fly, Harry?" Nan asked.

"Well, I read that one of the longest flights in the United States was made by an Army bird," Harry replied. "He flew over two thousand miles from Maine to Texas."

"I didn't know there were pigeons in the Army!" Freddie chimed in.

"If *I* were a pigeon!" Flossie said with a giggle, "I'd fly around the world!"

The others laughed. At that moment the telephone rang in the hall. Martha answered it and came to the door of the dining room to say the call was for Uncle Daniel.

"Hello," the children heard him say as he lifted the receiver.

There was a pause, then he gave a startled exclamation. After a short conversation, the farmer came back into the dining room.

"Is something the matter, Daniel?" Aunt Sarah asked.

"The Meadowbrook Bank has been robbed!" he replied.

"When?"

"Did they catch the robbers?" Questions came thick and fast from the twins and Harry.

Uncle Daniel held up his hand for silence. He explained that the guard had come upon the robbers just as they were leaving the bank with several sacks of money.

"Then he saw what they looked like!" Harry exclaimed excitedly.

His father shook his head. "No, he didn't. The two men wore masks. But he did chase the men and see them get into an old green car which was parked beside the bank."

"Did he notice which way they went?" Bert asked.

"The guard didn't, but the town police on

their way to answer the alarm call did. They said the car was heading in this direction!"

"Come on!" Freddie called, jumping up and starting for the front door. "Let's set up a roadblock!"

"Freddie! Come back here!" Aunt Sarah called out. But she was too late. All the children were out of the house and running down the lane toward the road.

"There they go!" Harry stopped and pointed as a car sped by, two men in the front seat.

"Let's follow them!" Freddie turned and ran back towards the farmhouse.

Uncle Daniel was standing in the doorway as the little boy, followed by the other children, reached the porch.

"We saw the robbers go by, Dad!" Harry cried. "Can't we chase them?"

Uncle Daniel looked uncertain. "But you don't know they were the bank robbers," he protested.

"It was a green car!" Nan insisted.

"And it was an old one," Bert added.

"Okay!" Uncle Daniel ran toward his station wagon parked in the driveway.

The children jumped in, and they sped down the lane!

CHAPTER IV

SEARCH FOR A CUB

"THERE'S the car!" Bert cried. He pointed to a speck which was quickly disappearing in the distance.

"Hurry, Dad!" Harry urged.

The farmer pressed his foot on the accelerator, and the station wagon leaped forward. There was no other traffic on the road, so Uncle Daniel managed to keep the distant car in sight. But finally they could see it no longer, because rain had begun to fall. Uncle Daniel slowed his car and came to a stop.

"Oh, don't give up!" Bert pleaded. "I *know* we can catch them!"

"I'm afraid not," his uncle replied. "They have too much of a head start!"

"Here comes a car behind us!" Nan observed.

The automobile stopped and a husky, dark-haired man in a uniform got out. He came up to the station wagon. "Oh, it's you, Mr. Bobbsey!" he exclaimed as he caught sight of Uncle Daniel.

"Lieutenant Kent!" the farmer cried. "Are you chasing the bank robbers too?"

"Yes. Have you seen them?"

"I don't know. We heard they escaped in an old green car and the children thought they saw the car go past the farm," Uncle Daniel explained. "We tried to follow it."

By this time another state policeman named Bennett had joined Lieutenant Kent. When Bennett heard the story, he went back to radio the information to headquarters.

Officer Kent told Uncle Daniel and the children that an alarm had gone out for the old green car. "Roadblocks have been set up all around the area. We're pretty sure these men are the same ones who robbed the banks in the other towns too."

"What makes you think so?" Uncle Daniel asked.

"Well, an old green car has been seen in each town just before the bank was robbed."

"I'm sorry we couldn't catch that car, if it did belong to the robbers," Uncle Daniel said.

"We're bound to find them sooner or later," Lieutenant Kent said as he started back to the police car.

"We'll keep looking for them, too!" Freddie called.

The troopers waved as they drove past the Bobbseys and on down the road. Uncle Daniel turned the wagon around and headed back to the farm.

"We've certainly had a 'citing first day in the country!" Flossie commented later when she and Nan were getting ready for bed.

"Yes," Nan agreed. "Bears and pigeons and bank robbers!" She turned out the light, and a minute later both girls were sound asleep.

After breakfast the next morning, Harry called the nearby headquarters of the State Police. Lieutenant Kent answered. He said that the green car had not been found. "And the bank robbers haven't been caught."

Harry told this to the others, then Bert, Freddie, and Harry went out to the barn. Nan and Flossie wandered into the kitchen.

"I was goin' to make a Dutch apple pie for dinner," Martha told them.

"Will you show me how to make it?" Nan asked eagerly. "I've never made one."

"Now's as good a time as any," Martha agreed, beginning to set out the flour, shortening, and other materials for the pastry.

Soon Nan had the dough ready to roll into

a crust. Flossie had settled herself at the big kitchen table with a bowl of apples. Dinah sat down to help her.

"Make apple curls, please, Dinah," Flossie begged.

Dinah chuckled and picked up an apple. Skillfully she peeled the fruit in one continuous piece. Then she handed Flossie the long curly peeling.

Snoop had just come into the kitchen. The cat put his front paws on Flossie's lap and stretched his face toward hers.

"Would you like to have some curls, Snoopie?" Flossie asked teasingly.

"Meow!" said the black cat.

By this time Dinah had another long peeling ready. With a giggle, Flossie put an apple curl over each of Snoop's pointed ears. The cat sneezed and shook his head, but the apple curls stayed on.

Snoop dropped to the floor. The apple peelings still clung to his ears. With his back arched and his legs stiff, the cat jumped straight up in the air. The peelings stayed on. The girls and women laughed at the funny sight.

"Here, Snoop, I'll take them off," Nan said soothingly. But the cat streaked from the room.

Martha, Dinah, Flossie, and Nan waited.

No sound came to their ears, but the next moment Snoop stalked through the kitchen. His curls were gone! He pushed open the screen door and went out.

"I guess he's mad at me, 'cause he knows boys don't wear curls," Flossie said, giggling as she took the bowl of sliced apples over to Nan.

"I'm sure he'll make up in a little while," Nan said.

She piled the apple slices into the sweetened pastry shell and topped them with butter and sugar and cinnamon. Then she placed the pie in the oven.

"You girls did a fine job," Martha complimented them. "I'll call you when the pie's baked."

Nan was impatient to see the pie. When Martha called a little later, she ran to the kitchen. Carefully she opened the oven door and pulled out the golden brown pie.

"Mmm! It smells good!" she said happily.

"It's a right nice-lookin' pie!" Martha said approvingly. "Just set it out on the back porch table so it'll cool quicker than in here."

Nan carried it out, then went back into the house to find Flossie. The little girl had gone upstairs to dress her dolls. It was half an hour before the two girls entered the kitchen.

The room was empty. The voices of Martha and Dinah floated up from the basement where they seemed to be working in the preserve closet.

"Where's the pie, Nan?" Flossie asked, looking around the kitchen.

"Out on the porch," Nan replied as she pushed open the screen door. "Why—!" she said in bewilderment, "where is it?"

The table was empty!

"Maybe the pie fell on the floor," Flossie suggested.

"I don't see how it could have," Nan remarked. But she looked all around the porch. The pie was not there.

Sadly Nan turned back into the kitchen followed by Flossie. At the door Nan stopped in amazement. The pie was in the middle of the kitchen table.

"I'm sure it wasn't there before!" she protested.

At that moment the girls heard a chuckle. They looked up in time to see a boy's head disappear around the closing door into the dining room. Nan ran to the door and flung it open.

There, doubled over with laughter, were Bert, Freddie, and Harry. "Bert Bobbsey!" Nan exclaimed. "You moved the pie!"

Still laughing, Bert admitted that he and the other two boys had taken the pie to tease the girls.

"Just for that, you may not get any of it to eat!" Nan threatened, but finally burst out laughing.

All the children were still giggling about the lost pie when Aunt Sarah bustled into the room. "Mr. Holden just telephoned," she said.

"Mrs. Holden's mother is very ill in California, and they're leaving for the West Coast immediately."

"That's too bad," Nan remarked sympathetically. "Are Tom and his little brother going with them?"

"Just Roy. I invited Tom to stay with us—"

"That will be great!" Harry interrupted.

His mother continued, "Mr. Holden can't leave the animals with no one there. A friend of his who is an animal trainer will come, but he can't arrive for a few days."

Dinah had come into the room while Aunt Sarah was talking. "Mrs. Bobbsey," she spoke up, "why don't you let old Dinah go over and take care of that boy while his daddy and mommy and brother are away?"

"We can help Tom with the animals until the man gets there," Bert added.

"Why, I think that's a wonderful plan!" Aunt Sarah said. "I'll call Mrs. Holden at once!"

The offer was quickly accepted. Dinah hurried upstairs to pack her bag, and Aunt Sarah went to get the station wagon. All the children piled in.

By the time the Bobbseys reached the neighboring farm, Mr. and Mrs. Holden and Roy were gone. Tom was feeding the animals.

Aunt Sarah went into the house with Dinah. The children followed Tom from cage to cage. When they reached the enclosure where the little bear cubs were kept, Tom stared in surprise.

"Where's Arthur?" he asked.

The Bobbseys ran up. Only four bears were romping in the pen. *Arthur was missing!*

"How dreadful!" cried Nan.

Tom said in a worried tone, "I don't know what Dad will say. As soon as he goes away, *I* lose one of the bears!"

Flossie slipped her hand into Tom's. "Don't worry," she said softly, "we'll find Arthur for you!"

"Sure!" Freddie agreed. "We're good at being 'tectives!"

The children scattered and began the search. Nan and Flossie walked up to the orchard while Harry and Bert went into the field behind the barn. Tom began a hunt around the animal enclosures.

"What would a real detective do?" Freddie asked himself. He thought a minute. "He'd look for tracks!"

The little boy walked slowly up the lane, peering carefully at the ground. Back of the house he came to a dirt path. Because of the rain the night before, the path was muddy.

"Prints!" Freddie exclaimed. He bent down and examined the tiny tracks in the wet earth. "They're a bear's!" he decided. "Five toes and the claw marks show, just the way Harry said they do!"

Freddie looked around. The other children had disappeared. "I'll find Arthur all by myself!" he told himself proudly.

The path ran along the edge of a field for a short distance, then turned into the woods. The little boy followed it, keeping his eyes on the tracks. Sometimes wet leaves covered the path, and he lost the prints. But each time he was able to pick them up again. He followed the trail for some time. Then the tracks disappeared.

Freddie looked up. He was surrounded by tall trees, and he could not see any path.

Suddenly his lower lip quivered as a dreadful idea came to him. "I'm lost!" he thought.

CHAPTER V

A SURPRISING CAPTURE

WHEN Freddie realized he was lost, he sat down on a log to think.

"I wonder where the path went?" the little boy asked himself. "I guess I haven't been on it for a long time!"

After a moment Freddie decided to try to find it. He got up and began to push his way among the bushes.

"Oh, there it is!" he told himself, after going a short way. By now, however, he was very confused.

"Which way did I come?" he thought, looking up the path. Then he noticed the tiny footprints leading off to his right.

"That's the way I was going!" he told himself. "I'll follow the tracks just a little farther. Then, if I don't find Arthur, I can turn around and go back!"

Freddie trudged ahead. Suddenly he stopped. Just a few yards beyond, in the middle of the trail, sat a little animal! It was black with a bushy tail. Down its back ran a broad white stripe.

"I think I'll make friends with him," Freddie said.

At that moment there was a rustling in the bushes and Nan and Flossie stepped onto the path.

"Stop, Freddie!" called Nan. "Don't touch that animal! It's a skunk!"

"I know, but he looks like a nice one!" Freddie protested.

Nan reminded him that skunks, when frightened or angry, squirt out a fluid which has a very unpleasant odor.

"Oh!" said Freddie, turning obediently away. The little animal scooted off down the path. "I guess the skunk made those tracks I thought were Arthur's!"

Nan looked at the little footprints. "They do look like a bear's," she admitted, "but they're much smaller."

"Anyway we already found Arthur!" Flossie piped up. "He was sitting in one of the trees in the orchard!"

"How did you find *me?*" Freddie asked. "I thought I was lost in the forest."

"You *were* lost, till we found you," Flossie said with a giggle.

Nan explained that they had been looking for him everywhere. They had been walking at the edge of the woods when they had caught sight of Freddie's red cowboy shirt.

"You're really not very far into the forest!" Flossie told him.

"Aunt Sarah is waiting for us," Nan said. "We must get back to the house."

The three hurried along the path. The trip did not seem half so long to Freddie now as it had before.

When Freddie and the girls reached the Holden house, they found Bert and Harry already in the station wagon with Aunt Sarah. Freddie told them about his adventure.

"Wow!" Harry exclaimed. "It's a good thing Nan found you before you got close to that skunk!"

They piled into the car. Dinah and Tom waved good-by as the wagon started on.

"Come over again tomorrow!" Tom called.

Back at Meadowbrook Farm, Martha had a good dinner ready, and they all pronounced Nan's Dutch apple pie the best they had ever eaten. Bert asked if there was any news of the robbers, but Uncle Daniel shook his head.

Later, when the children wandered outdoors,

Nan remarked, "We've been here a whole day, and we haven't taken Rocket out once!"

"Why don't we harness him to the cart now and have a ride?" Bert proposed.

The other children thought this a good idea and ran toward the barn. Rocket was dozing in his stall, but when Harry took down the harness from the wall, the pony gave a welcoming neigh.

In a few minutes Harry had the harness on the Shetland pony and backed him into the traces of the basket cart. Bert said he would drive and picked up the reins. The others climbed in.

"Giddap!" Bert called.

The pony tossed his head and trotted smartly down the lane. At the end Bert turned onto the highway.

"We'd better drive on the back roads," Harry said. "Rocket doesn't like traffic very much."

At the next dirt road, Bert turned off. They jogged along for a couple of miles between vine-covered fences. Nan started a song and the others joined in.

Suddenly Bert stopped singing. "Look up ahead!" he cried.

"The old green car!" Nan exclaimed.

A battered-looking green automobile was parked on the grassy strip between the road and the fence. When the pony cart drew alongside it, Bert pulled on the reins, and Rocket stopped.

"It's the bank robbers'!" Freddie cried.

"Pull over to the side, Bert," Harry directed. "Let's look at the car."

Bert guided Rocket off the road and the children jumped out. They swarmed about the automobile.

"Money bags!" Nan whispered, pointing to several brown cloth bags on the back seat of the car. She reached in to pick one up.

"Don't touch them," Bert advised. "I think we should leave that to the police. We might spoil some fingerprints!"

Hastily Nan drew back her hand. "I guess you're right," she agreed. "But where do you think the robbers are? They must be somewhere around!"

"I see them!" Flossie cried. She pointed off across the field. In the distance the children saw two figures moving about.

"They're burying the treasure!" Freddie guessed, his blue eyes round with excitement.

"Let's capture them!" Harry proposed, starting toward the fence.

"Wait a minute!" Bert called. "We don't want them to see us. They'll run away."

The five children talked over the problem

and decided to circle around the two men, keeping out of sight as much as possible. Then at a given signal—Bert would wave a handkerchief—they would all jump out and capture the robbers.

"I'll take Freddie and Flossie and go along that fence to the right," Bert offered.

"Then Nan and I will creep up on the left," Harry said.

Bert tied Rocket's reins to a fence post, and the Bobbseys began to carry out their plan. Nan and Harry climbed over the fence and started along the left side of the field, being careful to keep in the shadow of the bushes which divided the fields.

"Come on!" Bert called to the younger twins as he jumped down into the field.

Flossie followed quickly, but when Freddie tried to drop from the fence, a jagged section caught in the pocket of his jeans. He hung there, helpless.

"Flossie!" Freddie whispered loudly. "I'm stuck!"

Flossie turned back to her twin. She climbed up on the fence and pulled Freddie's pocket free. He scrambled down, and the two ran after Bert.

As they approached stealthily, the children saw the two figures move toward a clump of bushes near the end of the field. They also noticed that Nan and Harry had reached a position opposite them.

Bert stood up and waved his handkerchief. The five children advanced on the two figures. When they drew near, Bert dashed forward and grabbed the arm of the shorter of the two. He wheeled about.

"Bud Stout!" Bert exclaimed.

"What's up, Bert?" the chunky boy asked. "Are you playing a game?"

Bert looked embarrassed, but he could not keep from chuckling. Bud Stout was a friend of Harry's and had often come to Meadowbrook Farm to play when the twins were visiting their cousin.

By this time Harry and Nan had also come up. "Bud and Ken Stout!" Harry hooted. "We thought you were the bank robbers!"

Bud, who somewhat resembled his last name, looked puzzled. "Bank robbers!" he repeated. "What are you talking about?"

Harry and Bert explained about the robbers and the green car.

Bud Stout chuckled. "My brother bought that car with the money he and I earned helping Dad this year."

"And we even thought we had found money bags on the back seat!" Bert remarked.

Bert dashed forward and grabbed his arm

"Those are sacks of popping corn! We came out to pick some berries for Mom," Bud explained.

Ken, a dark-haired boy of eighteen, looked a little worried. "I bought the car in town last week, so I'm sure it can't be the one the thieves were using. I just hope the state troopers don't think it is and try to arrest me."

"They probably have a better description of the robbers' green car than we do," Nan said comfortingly. "They'll know yours isn't the one!"

Bud and Ken picked up their buckets of berries and walked toward the road with the Bobbseys. When they reached it, Ken went to his car and brought back a small bag of corn.

"Try some of this," he said and grinned. "I'm sorry it isn't the stolen money!"

"This is better 'cause we can eat it!" Freddie spoke up.

With a wave the Stout brothers got in the green car and drove off. Bert untied Rocket. When the little pony realized he was headed for home, he trotted along at a good clip.

"Ooh! This is fun!" Flossie cried. Her yellow curls blew in the breeze as she gripped the side of the basket cart.

Without any direction from Bert, Rocket turned into the lane at Meadowbrook Farm and came to a stop at the door of the barn.

"Flossie and I will start the corn popping while you boys unharness Rocket," Nan offered.

"Okay," Harry agreed. "We won't be long."

Nan filled the big corn popper. By the time Harry, Bert, and Freddie came in from the barn, she was pushing it back and forth over the fire. *Crack! Pop!* The fluffy white kernels hit against the sides of the wire popper.

Bert took a turn holding the wire basket, while Flossie brought a big yellow bowl from the pantry and set it on the table. Then Nan got butter and put it in a pan on the stove to melt.

"Yum!" said Freddie. "It smells good! May I push the popper now?"

Bert gave up his place to the little boy. Then Flossie had a turn. Finally all the hard grains of corn had turned into fluffy white bits. Nan poured the popped corn into the bowl while Flossie brought the melted butter. Harry picked up a big salt shaker. As Flossie poured the butter over the corn, Harry added the salt.

"Now we can eat it," Freddie said eagerly.

"Aunt Sarah's on the front porch," Nan spoke up. "Let's take the corn out to her first."

Just as Bert picked up the bowl, there came a loud *crash* from the direction of the barn!

CHAPTER VI

THE MYSTERY CAR

"WHAT was that?" Nan asked, startled.

Harry dashed to the door, with the twins at his heels. The popcorn was forgotten.

"It's Upsetter!" Harry cried. "He's broken out of the pasture!"

"Who's Upsetter?" Nan asked as she reached her cousin's side.

"I forgot to tell you. He's an old ram Dad is keeping for a neighbor. We call him Upsetter because whenever he gets loose he upsets something! The last time he knocked over a pile of milk cans."

"I'll catch him!" Freddie cried, running toward the barnyard.

Harry caught the little boy by the arm. "Better stay here, Freddie," he cautioned. "That old ram can be ugly and dangerous!"

"Come with me, Freddie," Nan said. "You

and Flossie and I will wait here on the porch until Upsetter is caught."

"But I want to help!" Freddie protested.

Harry explained that Uncle Daniel had gone into town and his farm hand was working in one of the fields. Bert and Harry would take care of the escaped ram.

"Baa! Baa!" The big sheep trotted out of the barnyard and made for the house. Directly in his path was a pile of wooden crates. The ram raced toward them, his huge horns lowered.

Crash! The crates fell to the ground.

"We must stop Upsetter before he does any more damage!" Harry said desperately.

Bert picked up a coil of rope from the porch floor. Quickly he looped one end. Twirling it over his head, he approached the ram. Surprised, the animal came to a halt, pawing the ground with his forefeet.

Expertly Bert threw the rope, which settled around the sheep's neck. The animal stood still for a minute, then turned and began to run, pulling Bert after him!

"Oh, stop him! Stop him!" Flossie cried. "He'll hurt my brother!"

"Get some salt from the kitchen, Nan!" Harry directed. "Sheep love salt. Maybe we can halt Upsetter with that!"

Nan dashed into the house and returned

with a box of salt. Before Harry could stop her, she ran out into the lane. Upsetter had dragged Bert around the barnyard and was now nearing the house once more.

Nan dumped the contents of the salt box in the ram's path, then raced back to the porch. When the animal glimpsed the pile of white grains, he paused and sniffed. At once he began to lick up the salt!

"Oh, goody!" cried Flossie.

Harry joined his panting cousin. "Are you all right, Bert?" he asked.

"Sure. That was quite a run, though," he said when he had caught his breath.

"Upsetter looks quiet enough now," Harry observed. "Let's get him into the barn."

Harry took hold of the rope to which Bert was still clinging, and together the two boys led the now docile ram toward the barn.

"We'll tie him in this stall," Harry said. "I think he'll be all right here until Dad gets back from town."

That evening Tom Holden rode over to say that his father's friend, Amos Berg, had arrived to help with the animal farm.

"He got here much sooner than Dad thought he would," Tom said. "I don't need to stay home now, so how about a practice pigeon race tomorrow between one of my birds and one of yours, Harry? Remember, Nan, you and Flossie were going to stay at my loft, while Bert and Freddie help Harry."

"I remember. We'll do it," said Nan.

The twins were excited at the prospect. Shortly after breakfast, Nan and Flossie walked over to the Holden farm. Tom was waiting for them, holding a pigeon in a wicker basket.

"Your pigeon and Harry's don't come back to the same loft," Nan said in a puzzled tone. "How can you tell which one wins?"

Tom explained that the birds were released together. When each bird entered its home loft, the exact time was written down. Then the distance of the pigeon's flight was divided by the time it had taken the bird to reach the loft.

"In that way we can tell which pigeon made the fastest flight," Tom concluded. He took the two girls to the pigeon loft and showed them where his bird would enter.

"Don't note the time until the bird is actually inside the loft," he cautioned. "Then just write down the time it shows on this clock." He pointed to a large alarm clock hanging on the wall. "Harry and I will go to Meadowbrook after we release the pigeons. Call me there."

Tom said it would be at least half an hour until he and Harry could release their pigeons from a field the two boys had chosen, which was halfway between the two farms. While waiting, the girls went into the kitchen. Dinah was there washing the breakfast dishes.

Nan and Flossie helped Dinah dry the dishes, then Nan looked at the clock. "We'd better get back to the loft, Flossie," she said. "The pigeon will be on his way home!"

The girls stationed themselves on the flat roof by the loft with the clock plainly in sight. In a few minutes Flossie cried, "Here he comes!"

They watched as the gray-and-white bird made his way toward them. With a flutter of wings, he settled down on the landing platform in front of the trap door.

Flossie looked at the clock. "It's just ten-twenty!" she announced. "Write it down, Nan!"

"Tom said we should wait until the pigeon is inside the loft," Nan protested. She waved a hand at the bird, but it did not move!

It was nearly ten minutes later before the pigeon finally pushed open the trap door and entered the loft. Nan and Flossie ran into the house and telephoned Meadowbrook Farm.

Tom sounded disappointed when Nan told him his pigeon had refused to enter the trap. "Harry won that race, then," he said. "We're all coming over there," Tom continued. "Bert says for you and Flossie to wait for us."

"Let's take the father rabbit for a walk," Flossie suggested as the girls passed the animal pens a few minutes later.

"We can't take a rabbit on a leash like a dog!" Nan protested with a laugh.

"Sure we can!" Flossie insisted She ran back to the house and got a length of string from Dinah. When she returned to Nan, the little girl entered the pen. In another minute she had tied one end of the string around the rabbit's neck and was leading it out of the enclosure.

The little animal did not know what to make of the situation. He ran forward. When he was brought up short by the string, he sat down on the path and refused to budge. But as they entered the woods, he hopped ahead happily.

Suddenly Flossie felt a hard tug on the string. Then the rabbit disappeared! "Wh— where is he?" the little girl asked in bewilderment.

Nan pointed to a hole in the ground. "He ran down there," she said.

"I'll pull him out," Flossie announced, and gave the string a sharp tug. It snapped in two!

"O! We've lost Tom's rabbit!" Flossie cried in distress. "What will we do?"

Nan looked around her. "Maybe we can get some water and pour it down the hole to make him come out," she suggested.

The two girls pushed through the undergrowth until they came to a stream. They made a little bowl of several large leaves and filled it with water. Carefully Nan poured it down the rabbit hole.

"There he goes!" Flossie shrieked. "He ran out another way!"

Nan and Flossie started in pursuit, but they were no match for the rabbit. He vanished into the bushes. Flossie started to cry, and Nan was worried. What would Mr. Holden say?

Sadly the two girls began to retrace their steps. In a few minutes, they came to a fork in the path.

"We came this way," Flossie announced, and took the left turn. Nan looked doubtful, but her little sister had skipped ahead, so she followed.

They had gone only a little distance when Flossie cried out, "Oh, look at that poor rabbit! He's caught!"

By the side of the trail a large rabbit was struggling in a snare. Gently Nan released the panting animal and cradled it in her arms.

"Who could have been so mean?" Flossie asked, her blue eyes filling with tears.

"He's all right, but his paw is hurt a little bit," Nan said reassuringly. "We'll take him back and bandage it."

"I'm glad it wasn't Mr. Holden's rabbit," Flossie broke in.

"Oh, look at that poor rabbit!" Flossie cried

The girls walked on through the woods. Nan looked more and more puzzled. "I'm sure this isn't the way we came," she said finally, and peered ahead among the trees. "I think this path is leading out to a road."

In another minute Nan and Flossie stepped onto a rutted country road. Just then they saw a pigeon fly out of the woods and head straight up into the blue sky.

"Where did the pigeon come from?" Flossie asked in surprise. "Do you s'pose it's one of Tom's?"

"If it is, I wish we could fly and follow it," Nan said with an uncertain laugh. "I don't know which way the Holdens' farm is!"

She gazed upward. "I remember when we started out the sun was in front of us. So I guess it should be back of us on the way home!"

Flossie followed as Nan turned to her right and started up the road. They walked along in silence for a few minutes. Then Flossie pointed to a car parked at the edge of the woods.

"There's Bud Stout's brother's car," she exclaimed. "Maybe they set that trap for the rabbit!"

"Well, it's a mean thing to do!" Nan replied indignantly. "I'm glad we found it!"

"I see Tom's house!" Flossie cried out happily a short time later. "Mr. Sun showed us the way home!"

When the girls walked up the farmhouse lane, they found the four boys waiting for them.

"We thought you were lost!" Bert cried. "Dinah didn't know where you had gone!"

"We lost a rabbit and found another!" Flossie cried. "Tom, will your father be awfully, awfully mad at us for taking Daddy Rabbit for a walk and letting him run away?"

Tom looked at the animal Nan was carrying. "You've sure got a big one there," he said with a grin. "He's even better than the one you lost."

Tom introduced the girls to Amos Berg, a thin, dark-haired man, with twinkling blue eyes. He took the rabbit from Nan and promised to bandage the injured paw.

"Here comes Bud Stout," Harry said as the stocky boy strolled into the farmyard.

"Hi, Bud!" Nan called. "We just passed your car on the back road."

Bud grinned. "You didn't see our car! It broke down right after we left you yesterday. It's in town being fixed."

Nan looked startled. "Then the one we saw must have been the bank robbers' car!" she cried.

CHAPTER VII

MARK'S TRICK

"THE bank robbers!" Freddie exclaimed. "Where? Let's get them!"

Like a flash the little boy ran down the lane, with the other Bobbseys after him. When he reached the main road, Freddie stopped. "Which way?" he asked Flossie.

"Over there on that little road alongside the woods," his sister directed.

The children ran on, following the girl's directions. Finally Nan paused and looked around. "I think the car was parked here," she said, "but it's gone!"

"Then let's look around for clues," Bert said.

He walked slowly along the side of the road studying the ground. The others also searched. Freddie even got down on his hands and knees to examine the dirt near where Nan said the green car had been parked. The ground was dry and no tire tracks showed up clearly.

Finally Bert straightened. "I guess we're not going to find any clues here!" he said in a discouraged tone.

Suddenly Nan asked, "Bud, did you see any men when you set the rabbit snare?"

"What are you talking about?" Bud asked, bewildered. "I didn't set any snare!"

"This is getting complicated," said Bert. "What's the story?"

Nan told about finding the rabbit caught in the woods.

"I haven't been in the woods this morning," Bud protested. He laughed. "You kids are bound to make a bad guy out of me!"

"I'm terribly sorry," said Nan. She smiled. "You're not. I think you're tops!"

Freddie was getting tired of this kind of talk. "I'm hungry!" he said. "Let's go!"

Harry laughed and patted his cousin on the head. "So am I! We'd better get back to Meadowbrook. Martha will have dinner ready and wonder where we are!"

The Bobbseys started off, then Harry turned back to Tom and Bud. "Why don't you two fellows come over this afternoon?" he suggested. "We're going to pick apples, and you can help!"

"Sure thing," Tom replied.

"Count on me!" Bud agreed. "You have the best apples around here. I may even eat a few!"

After dinner Harry and the twins went up to the orchard where Uncle Daniel and a number of pickers were working.

"Where shall we start, Dad?" Harry asked his father.

"Take these two rows." Uncle Daniel pointed out the trees at the edge of the orchard. "Freddie and Flossie," he added, "be careful when you climb the ladders. We don't want any broken twins!"

The small twins giggled as they picked up two baskets and walked over to the trees. They had just scrambled up the small step ladders and set the baskets on the top, when they heard Harry give a low whistle.

"Look who's coming up the lane with Bud and Tom!" he said. "Mark Teron!"

As the three boys drew near, Bud left the others and hurried up to Harry. "Is it all right if Mark picks too?" he asked. "He came over to my house, and I couldn't shake him."

"Sure!" Harry replied good-naturedly. "Just as long as he doesn't make trouble!"

The newcomers took baskets, and each went to a tree. Mark began to work on the one next to Freddie. For a while the children picked steadily, filling their baskets with the colorful fruit.

Then Mark began to slow down. He looked over at Freddie, who was picking busily. "Hey, Freddie," Mark called, "aren't you eating any of those apples?"

The little boy looked up and grinned. "Sure, I ate one," he replied.

"One!" Mark pretended to be shocked. "Don't you know that eating apples makes you strong? You'll never grow up if you don't eat more than that!"

"I'll eat a couple more!" Freddie promised eagerly, impressed by Mark's knowledge.

"I'll tell you what we'll do!" Mark cried. "We'll have an apple-eating contest—just the two of us!"

"Okay!" Freddie picked a greenish apple. "I'll start with this one!"

Mark picked an apple too and bit into it. When it was finished, he took another. "Hurry up, Freddie!" he called. "I'm getting ahead of you!"

Quietly, when Freddie was not looking, Mark dropped the second apple into his basket. This went on, with Freddie eating apples as fast as he could get them down and Mark urging him on.

Finally Freddie paused, a peculiar look on his chubby face. "I—I feel funny!" he stammered.

At that moment Flossie looked over from her perch by the next tree. She saw her twin sway as he tried to climb down his ladder.

"Nan!" she shrieked. "Something's the matter with Freddie!"

Nan rushed over and caught Freddie as he reached the ground. "What's wrong?" she asked anxiously.

"Mark and I were playing an apple-eating game!" Freddie said weakly. "But I can't eat any more. My tummy aches!"

Nan looked indignantly at Mark, who was smiling. "If this is your idea of a joke, Mark Teron," Nan stormed, "I think you're pretty mean!"

"Aw, Freddie'll be all right!" Mark said scornfully. "It's not my fault if he ate too many apples!"

With a parting glare at Mark, Nan led Freddie toward the farmhouse. They were met at the door by Aunt Sarah. When Nan explained what had happened, her aunt insisted that Freddie go to bed at once.

Freddie felt too bad to protest. In another minute he was tucked between the cool sheets. He closed his eyes wearily.

When Flossie saw Nan taking her twin into the house, she hurriedly climbed down her ladder. Leaving her basket of apples at the foot of the tree, she ran after her brother and sister.

"Is Freddie terrible sick?" she asked anxiously when Nan and Aunt Sarah came downstairs.

Aunt Sarah hugged her little niece. "He ate too much. He'll feel better after a while."

Aunt Sarah went out to the kitchen, and Nan ran back to the orchard.

Flossie stood in the hall, thinking. "Freddie needs a nurse," she decided. "I'll take care of him!"

Flossie ran upstairs to her room. She took a fresh white handkerchief from the bureau drawer and pinned it over her blond curls. Then she rummaged among the playthings which she had brought to Meadowbrook and pulled out a toy stethoscope. She hung this around her neck.

"Now I'm a nurse," Flossie observed with satisfaction as she looked in the mirror.

She tiptoed down the hall and peeked into Freddie's room. The little boy seemed to be sleeping.

"I'll get some cold water and bathe his face," the little nurse told herself. "That's what Mommy does when I don't feel good."

In the bathroom she filled a glass with water and picked up a towel. When she reached the boys' room again, Flossie tiptoed across the polished floor toward the bed. She stood quietly on a small hooked rug beside it.

In a moment Freddie's twin dipped one end of the towel into the glass of water and bent over Freddie. As she did, the rug skidded and her feet slipped. She fell hard onto the bed. The water flew out of the glass right onto Freddie's face!

"Wh-wh-!" he spluttered, sitting up quickly. He mopped his face with the end of the sheet. "What are you doing, Flossie?" he asked.

His twin just stared. "I'm your nurse. I was only going to bathe your face. I didn't mean to spill the water all over you!"

"That's all right," Freddie said generously. "I prob'ly need a face wash!"

"Now that you're awake, I'll play some music," Flossie remarked, snapping on the little radio by the bedside.

They were just in time to hear the beginning of a local newscast. "The Meadowbrook Bank, which was robbed day before yesterday," the announcer said, "is offering a reward of five hundred dollars to be paid to anyone providing information leading to the arrest of the robbers."

"Wh-wh—!" Freddie spluttered

Freddie sat up and swung his legs over the edge of the bed. "Five hundred dollars!" he exclaimed. "We've got to find those bad men, Flossie!"

"But you're sick!" his twin protested.

"I'm well now," Freddie stated. He thought a minute. "If we're going to be detectives, we'll have to look different from the way we do now."

Flossie giggled. "I know what we can do!"

"What?"

"We can change clothes with each other! I'll be Freddie and you can be Flossie!"

Flossie ran to her room and returned with a pink-and-white checkered dress. It had a full skirt and no sleeves. Freddie handed her a pair of pants and a shirt. While she went to put them on, Freddie slipped on the dress. When his twin returned, she stood back to inspect him.

"Your head looks funny," Flossie decided. She hurried off and came back with a pink ribbon, which she tied around Freddie's curly blond hair.

At that moment Bert, Nan, and Aunt Sarah came up the stairs. "Apple picking's all over!" Nan sang out. "How are you feeling, Fred—"

As his sister came into the bedroom, she

stopped talking. Bewildered, Nan looked from one child to the other. "Why—why—" she stuttered, "which is which?"

Flossie laughed in delight. "I'm Freddie! We're changing places. Then we're going to catch the bank robbers and win a lot of money!"

Aunt Sarah dropped into a chair. "What on earth are you talking about, child?" she asked.

Flossie had run from the room again, but Freddie explained about the radio broadcast and the reward of five hundred dollars. When his twin returned, she carried a doll.

"There!" she said, putting the doll in Freddie's arms before he could protest. "Now you're Flossie Bobbsey!"

At the sight of Freddie in the full-skirted dress hugging the doll, the older twins and Aunt Sarah burst into laughter. In disgust Freddie threw the doll on the bed and tore off the hair ribbon.

"I'm not going to play that game!" he cried, his face turning red with embarrassment. "Go out, everybody, while I put on my own clothes!"

As they left the room, the telephone rang. Harry answered it in the lower hall. In a few minutes he came to the others in the living room.

"Bud Stout has some great news for us!" he announced.

CHAPTER VIII

MOUNTAIN CAMPERS

THE others looked at Harry expectantly. "What's the big news?" Bert demanded.

"Mr. Stout has invited us to go camping tomorrow," Harry said. "We'll stay out overnight!"

Freddie jumped up from the table in his excitement. "Yippee!" he cried. "I'm going to sleep outdoors!"

Aunt Sarah smiled. "That's very nice of Mr. Stout," she said. "How are you going?"

"Mr. Stout will drive us in his farm truck," Harry answered. "Tom Holden is going, and Bud has asked Patty Manners and Kim Harold so Nan and Flossie won't be the only girls."

"Terrific!" Nan said. "I like Patty and Kim."

The two girls were about Nan's age, and she

had become friendly with them on previous visits to Meadowbrook.

"We'll have a great time!" said Bert.

The children went to bed early. Freddie dreamed that a big black bear was nuzzling him in his sleeping bag. He thrust out an arm to push the animal away and opened his eyes. Bert was seated on the edge of his bed, trying to shake his brother awake. It was morning!

"Come on, Freddie!" Bert urged. "Everyone else is already downstairs!"

The little boy jumped out of bed and hurried into his clothes. By the time Mr. Stout drove up in the truck, the five Bobbsey children were ready and waiting.

"Hi, Nan! Hi, Flossie!" called Patty Manners, a freckle-faced girl with dark curly hair.

"Isn't this going to be fun?" asked blond Kim, showing her dimples.

Nan joined her in the front seat while the others climbed into the back. They stepped over piles of sleeping bags and other camping gear to reach two long seats which had been placed across the truck body.

Uncle Daniel came out to talk to Mr. Stout. Conversation turned to the bank robbers. "Despite the children's clue about the green car they saw, the police haven't captured the men yet."

"So we should still keep looking," said Bert. "While we're riding, everybody look for a green car."

"You bet," Freddie piped up.

Uncle Daniel asked Mr. Stout, "Where are you taking these Indian campers?"

"I thought we'd go up to Boulder Lake," the sandy-haired man answered. "No one camps there much because of the long walk in from the road, but the children will enjoy it.

"Actually it isn't far from here as the crow flies," Mr. Stout continued, "but it will take us most of the day going by road."

"Does the pigeon fly the same way?" Flossie asked.

Mr. Stout laughed. "I guess a pigeon would take the shortest way too!" he replied. "That's what we mean when we say 'as the crow flies.'"

"Oh," said Flossie.

The children waved and shouted good-by to Uncle Daniel and Aunt Sarah, and the truck started down the lane.

"Start watching for any signs of those bank robbers," Bert reminded the others.

"Sure!" said Tom. "And maybe we can find some more small animals for our animal farm."

"I'll find you a big, wild one!" Freddie boasted.

The boys and girls had a good time as the

truck rolled along. They sang and told jokes and riddles until it was time to stop for a picnic lunch which Aunt Sarah and Martha had prepared.

All morning and also after lunch, the Bobbseys kept a sharp lookout for the green car or any suspicious-looking men. But they saw neither.

About three o'clock Mr. Stout drove up a steep, rocky road and parked under a tree. "End of the line!" he called. "Everybody out!"

"But I don't see any lake!" Flossie cried in disappointment as she looked around the stony landscape dotted with pine trees.

"The road doesn't go any farther," Bud told her. "We have to walk in to the lake."

Under Mr. Stout's direction, each of the children picked up a load from the truck and began the long walk. The group scrambled over rocks until they came to a wooded section.

"We'll be at Boulder Lake any minute," Bud promised.

"I see it! I see it!" Freddie shouted, running ahead. The lake, surrounded by tall pine trees, was small. Its shores were covered with boulders.

"Look at all the rocks!" Nan exclaimed.

"I think it's bee-yoo-ti-ful!" Flossie cried.

Mr. Stout told the twins that Boulder Lake

was almost on top of a stony mountain not far from Meadowbrook. He pointed toward one end of the lake. "The farm is down there beyond those woods."

Harry looked at the sky. "A storm's coming," he observed. "We'd better get our camp set up!"

Mr. Stout walked over to a level area just above the rocky lake shore. "This looks like a good spot," he observed.

Bud's father explained that he had brought three tents. "The largest will be for the four girls. Then I thought Bert, Harry, and Freddie could bunk together. Tom, Bud, and I will occupy the third."

It did not take long to set up the tents. The girls tossed their sleeping bags into their "house," then crept in themselves.

Kim Harold pulled a bathing suit from her bag. "Who wants to go swimming?" she asked.

"I think we'd better wait until we see if it's going to storm," Nan observed. "The wind seems pretty strong."

She had hardly spoken, when a sudden violent gust blew in off the lake. It lifted the tent into the air and then dropped it directly over the four girls!

"Help! Help!" they cried in muffled tones.

Mr. Stout and the boys dashed to their rescue. In a minute they had pulled the canvas aside,

and the girls crawled out from under it.

"Ooh!" Flossie exclaimed, taking a deep breath of air. "It was spooky under there!"

Mr. Stout looked sternly at Bud. "You'll have to put up a tent better than that, son, if you want to be a good camper!"

"It was partly my fault, sir," Tom Holden spoke up. "I didn't pound the stakes in far enough!"

The boys got busy and set up the tent again. This time they were careful to see that the pegs were firmly fastened into the ground. Then as an added precaution, they placed heavy stones on the edge of the canvas to weight it down.

Mr. Stout examined all the tents and pronounced them safe. By now the wind had died down. The black clouds had gone and the sky was blue again.

"Anybody hungry?" Mr. Stout asked.

"Yes!" the children chorused.

"We're going to have ham and pancakes," Bud explained. "And here is our griddle." He held up a large flat rock. "We'll need four small stones to put this on."

Bert and Freddie found the stones. They laid one under each corner of the flat stone. Then a fire was built under the griddle. While Kim and Flossie placed the ham slices on the stone, Nan and Patty mixed the pancake batter in a big pitcher.

In a few minutes the appetizing odor of sizzling ham filled the air. On another large flat rock, Bud and his father set out tin plates, knives and forks, butter, and maple syrup.

By this time the ham was cooked. Nan put the slices on a plate and poured rounds of batter on the hot griddle.

"Come and get it!" Mr. Stout called a short time later.

The children needed no urging. They picked up plates and helped themselves.

"I'll cook the pancakes for a while, Nan," Harry volunteered.

"We'll all take turns," Bert spoke up.

"This is yummy!" Flossie said as she put another pancake on her plate and poured syrup over it. Bud passed around pears for dessert, and some cookies.

The campers spent a long time eating. When they finished, the sun had set and darkness was beginning to cover the camp site. The fire glowed cheerfully.

With heavy gloves, Mr. Stout lifted the stone griddle off the fire. While the girls washed the plates in the lake, the boys brought more wood and built a roaring fire.

Presently Bert walked down to the edge of the lake and peered off in the direction of Meadowbrook. Up here on the mountain, the farm seemed very far away.

Suddenly he called to Harry, "Come here a minute!"

When his cousin had joined him, Bert

pointed down the rocky side of the mountain. "See those lights?" he asked. "I wonder what they are."

"Looks like a campfire," Harry guessed. "See how the light flickers."

"But Bud said no one ever camps up here," Bert objected.

"That light is pretty far away," Harry said. "It's much nearer Meadowbrook than we are."

The sound of singing around the campfire drew the boys back to the others. The strange lights were forgotten.

Some time later Nan glanced over at Flossie. The little girl was fast asleep, her curly head resting against a tree trunk. In her hand were several cookies. When the singing stopped, Flossie got up drowsily and stumbled toward her tent.

Mr. Stout stood up. "Flossie has the right idea!" he said with a smile. "I suggest we *all* climb into our sleeping bags."

In another ten minutes, all was quiet in the camp except for the sound of the water lapping against the boulders on the lake shore.

Flossie had fallen asleep again as soon as she had snuggled down into her sleeping bag. But suddenly she awakened. Something was crouching alongside her pillow!

CHAPTER IX

A SUSPICIOUS CORNFIELD

"NAN!" Flossie whispered desperately. Her sister did not stir. "Nan, wake up!" Flossie repeated.

"Wh—what is it?" Nan murmured sleepily.

"There's something by my pillow. I'm afraid to move!"

Nan reached for her flashlight. She switched it on and turned the light toward Flossie. There by the pillow squatted a little fat furry animal. He was nibbling the cookies which Flossie had laid down beside her.

"It's an opossum!" Nan exclaimed.

Her voice frightened the animal, which ran off in a hurry.

"I wish he'd stayed!" Flossie said sorrowfully. "I'd like to play with him!"

"Go back to sleep, honey," Nan advised. "Maybe we can find him in the morning."

The next thing the girls heard was the sound of the four older boys whistling reveille. "Come on, sleepyheads!" Bert called. "Don't you want any breakfast?"

The four girls scrambled from their beds, and in a few minutes joined the boys by the campfire.

"We're having fried egg sandwiches," Bud Stout said. "They're a Stout specialty!"

Mr. Stout walked down to the lake and returned with a mesh bag filled with cans of fruit juice which had been cooling in the cold water. While he opened the cans and passed them around, Bud fried bacon on the stone griddle.

"Where are the egg sandwiches?" Bert asked.

"Wait!" Bud took several slices of bread and tore holes in the centers. He put the bread on the hot griddle and broke an egg into each hole. When the egg had set, he deftly turned it and the bread over.

"There they are!" he said a minute later as he slipped the sandwiches off the stone and onto the plates. "We call them bulls' eyes!"

"Say! That's neat!" Freddie said admiringly.

"And good!" Patty Manners added.

As they all sat around the campfire eating their breakfast, Freddie said, "Quiet, everybody! I want to see if I can catch that chipmunk over there."

The little brown animal, with two black stripes running down its back, was seated at the foot of a tree, its bright eyes watching the campers curiously.

"Here, Freddie." Mr. Stout handed him a peanut. "Maybe he'd like this."

Freddie held the nut toward the little animal. "Here, Chippy," he called softly. "Come get your breakfast."

At first the chipmunk did not move. But Freddie sat very quietly, holding out the nut. Finally the animal scampered up to him and grabbed the morsel. Back under the tree again, he sat up on his haunches and nibbled busily.

The next time Freddie offered a nut, the little chipmunk did not hesitate. He took it from his hand and sat nearby to eat it. Carefully Freddie reached out and picked him up.

"I'm going to take him back for Mr. Holden!" the little boy announced, his blue eyes shining.

"Put him in this." Bud handed him an empty cracker box.

Shortly after that, the camping gear was divided among the children, and the hike back to the truck began. Soon they were winding down the mountain.

"Remember those lights we saw last night?" Bert asked Harry.

His cousin nodded. "They could have been around here some place."

Bert made a quick decision. "Mr. Stout," he called up to the driver, "may we stop here?"

The farmer pulled over to the side of the road. "Sure. Anything the matter?" he asked.

Bert told about the lights which he and Harry had noticed the night before. "They might possibly have belonged to the bank robbers," he said. "I'd like to look around a little."

"Okay." Mr. Stout smiled. "Bud tells me you're quite a detective! I'll go along and learn how you do it."

"All of us twins like to solve mysteries," Nan spoke up.

Everyone climbed out of the truck and began to scramble over the rocks and into the woods.

Suddenly Tom stopped. "There are some deer tracks!" he said. He pointed to marks in the damp earth.

"They look like two flower petals," Flossie remarked.

Tom told her that deer are called toenail walkers because, like all hoofed animals, they walk on their toenails. "The tracks are always easy to spot," he concluded.

"Here are some human footprints!" Bert called out excitedly.

"Let's follow them!" Nan suggested.

The prints were of two sizes, one set much narrower than the other. They led through a small clearing, then into the woods again. The children hurried along eagerly. In a few minutes they came to a rocky area.

"We've lost the prints!" Bud said. "They don't show on this stone."

"What a funny-looking rock!" Flossie pointed to a large pointed boulder which reared up before them.

"It looks like a giant lemon-drop candy standing on end!" Freddie remarked.

Bert considered the strange-shaped boulder. "If I could climb to the top, I'd have a good view down into the valley. Maybe I could see the men who left these footprints!"

"I'll give you a boost!" Harry volunteered.

With his help Bert managed to find several footholds and clawed his way to the top of the high rock. Shading his eyes he gazed over the surrounding countryside.

"I don't see anyone," he said finally.

"You may as well come down then," Mr. Stout advised.

Bert looked at the ground. It was almost a sheer drop from his perch on the boulder, and no one could reach up to him.

"It didn't seem so bad getting here," Bert said, "but I don't know how I'm going to get down!"

Nan looked worried. "It's too far to jump. You'd hurt yourself, Bert!"

"If you were in a fire, you could jump into a net!" Freddie remarked.

"A net! Of course!" Nan looked relieved. "We'll hold a blanket and you can jump into it."

"But we haven't a blanket!" Flossie objected.

"I'll get one from the truck," Harry said, and turned to run back to the road. The other boys followed him.

Bert sat down on top of the boulder. "I may as well make myself comfortable," he joked.

The girls stood at the base of the rock and talked to him. Finally, after what seemed like a long time, the boys returned. Bud spread out the blanket. Harry, Tom, and he, each picked up a corner while Mr. Stout took the fourth.

"I want to help!" Freddie protested.

"You hold the blanket on the side here between Bud and me," Mr. Stout directed.

"Okay, Bert!" Freddie called up. "We're ready!"

"Jump when I count three," Mr. Stout instructed.

"Okay, Bert," Freddie called. "We're ready!"

Bert nodded.

"One! Two! Three!"

Bert crouched and let himself drop into the outstretched blanket. His weight made the boys stagger, but they held on tightly. Bert bounced up once. Then they let the blanket fall to the ground, and Bert rolled off onto the rocks.

"Thanks a million," he said gratefully as he got to his feet. "I might have been stuck up there for hours!"

"It was good practice for being a fireman," Freddie observed. The small twin had said ever since babyhood that he was going to be a fireman when he grew up.

It was late in the afternoon when the Stout truck finally drew near Meadowbrook. Bert and Freddie were in the front seat with Mr. Stout.

"Why is that car parked across the road?" Bert suddenly asked, peering ahead.

Mr. Stout slowed the truck. "It looks like a roadblock," he said. "I wonder what's happened."

"Maybe it's for the bank robbers," guessed Freddie.

As they came close, they could see it was a state trooper's car. Another stood beside a cornfield, while still a third blocked off traffic from the far end.

The occupants of the truck heard a loud call. "Come out of there! We know you're in that field!"

Mr. Stout halted the truck, and the children jumped out. Bert and Harry ran up to the trooper who stood in the road with a loud-speaker in his hand. They recognized Lieutenant Kent.

"What's up?" Harry asked.

Trooper Kent turned to the boys. "A man up the road reported seeing two men run into this cornfield. They haven't come out, and we think they may be the bank robbers."

The corn was high, and any number of men could easily have hidden among the tall stalks. The trooper raised the speaker to his mouth again.

"Just walk out, and there won't be any trouble!" he called.

Everyone waited anxiously, but nobody emerged from the cornfield.

"Maybe the men ran out the other side of the field," Nan suggested.

"I don't think so," the policeman replied. "We have the whole field surrounded."

"Harry and I'll go in and find the men for you," Bert volunteered eagerly.

"Tom and I want to go too!" Bud spoke up.

The state policeman smiled. "Thanks for

offering to help, but I can't let you boys go in there. It's too dangerous. Those men may be armed!"

"How are you going to get them out?" Nan asked.

The trooper explained that at a pre-arranged signal, the police would move into the field from all sides. They expected this would make the fugitives in the field give up.

At that moment three shrill whistles sounded. "That's it!" Lieutenant Kent cried. He signaled the other troopers on the road. They walked stealthily into the cornfield.

"Ooh, this is scary, isn't it?" Flossie said with a little shiver.

The children listened eagerly for any sign of struggle in the cornfield. They heard nothing.

After about fifteen minutes, the corn stalks near the road began to wave back and forth.

"Here comes someone!" Freddie said excitedly. "Maybe it's a robber!"

As if in reply, five state troopers stepped from the field. They were led by Officer Bennett.

"Didn't you find anyone?" Bert asked, running toward the policeman.

"No. We've gone through that field from all directions. We can't find anyone," the state trooper replied.

Lieutenant Kent joined them. "I guess that was a false alarm. We'll lift the roadblock. You folks can go on."

Harry and the twins had a great deal to tell Uncle Daniel and Aunt Sarah when they reached home. They had just finished their exciting story when Tom Holden telephoned. Nan answered.

"Something terrible has happened!" he told her.

CHAPTER X

YOUNG TRAPPERS

TOM was so excited that his voice shook. "I'm sure I know who did it, too!"

"Did what, Tom?" Nan asked.

"Someone opened the cages. All our animals are gone!"

"How terrible! Wasn't Amos there? Didn't he see anyone?"

By this time the other children had run into the hall where Nan was talking. She turned from the telephone and told them the news.

Bert took the receiver from her. "Who do you think did it, Tom?" he asked.

Tom explained that Amos Berg had driven to town to buy more food for the animals. When he returned, he had found all the cage doors open and the animals gone. Dinah had not noticed anyone near the cages.

"I'll bet Mark Teron did it!" Tom went on. "He was mad because Bud didn't invite him to go camping with us. He knew you Bobbseys were helping me with the animals and thought this would be a good way to get even with us!"

"You really shouldn't accuse him unless you're sure, Tom," said Bert soberly.

"Well, I'm going to call him and ask him about it!" Tom promised defiantly. "I'll let you know what he says."

A few minutes later Tom called back. He sounded apologetic. "I guess I was wrong about Mark," he admitted. "When I called him, Mrs. Teron said he left early yesterday morning to visit his grandmother for a few days, so he couldn't have let the animals out."

"Have you notified the police?" Harry asked.

"Yes. Amos called Trooper Headquarters. None of the animals is really dangerous, but the bears might frighten people!"

Bert got on the line. "We'll come over in the morning, Tom," he promised, "and help you look for clues. It's too dark to see now."

Tom sounded relieved. "Thanks, Bert. I'll see you tomorrow."

The Bobbseys hurried through breakfast the next morning. After Flossie and Nan had made the beds, and Bert and Freddie had helped Harry with the outdoor chores, they started for the Holden farm.

Tom was standing at the end of the lane waiting for them. "Hi!" he called. "The state troopers have just left."

"Did they find out anything?" Bert asked.

Tom shook his head. "No. They can't decide whether the cages were simply opened by a trickster, or whether the animals were actually stolen."

"If they *were* let out as a joke," Bert theorized, "most of the animals would have just wandered into the woods. And if anyone saw a bear loose, I should think he would report it."

"Let's look around and see if we can find any clues," Nan suggested.

The ground around the cages had been so trampled that it was impossible to distinguish any prints.

"If the animals ran into the woods, maybe we can find some prints in there," Harry remarked.

The children searched carefully all along the edge of the woods, but found no animal tracks. They returned to the cages.

"Here's a great big skunk track," Freddie cried suddenly.

The others ran to look. Tom was excited. "I'm sure that's a bear track!" he cried. "And look, it goes out to the road!"

"Do you think all the animals escaped along the road?" Nan asked doubtfully.

"Who knows?" Tom sighed.

"Let's ask around and see if anyone saw animals on the loose," Bert proposed.

"Okay," Tom agreed. "It's worth a try."

The children started down the road toward the next farm. No one there had noticed any stray animals. When the children reached the road again, the rural mailman was just putting some letters inside the mailbox.

"What are you youngsters doing? Going for a hike?" he asked with a smile.

Tom explained about the missing animals. "Did you see any of them on the road yesterday?" he asked.

The mailman laughed. "If I'd seen any bears walking along the road yesterday, I would have reported it, before delivering another letter!"

Then he looked thoughtful. "Come to think of it," he said, "I did see a suspicious-looking truck around here yesterday."

"What do you mean?" Nan asked eagerly.

"Well," the postman said, "the driver was going very slowly, looking at all the names on the mailboxes. But when I stopped and asked if I could help him, he just speeded off."

"Do you suppose someone stole the animals and took them away in a truck?" Tom asked in bewilderment.

"Oh, poor Arthur!" Flossie cried.

The children could do no more. They walked sadly back to the Holden farm and told Amos Berg what they had discovered.

"Tom's father is goin' to be awful upset when he gets back and finds all his animals gone!" Amos said sadly.

"Let's capture some other animals for the animal farm!" Freddie proposed.

The others thought this a splendid idea. Amos went into the barn and returned with several wire traps—one for each child. He explained that these traps would not hurt the animals.

"You just bait them here in the middle," he said. "Then when the animal walks in to get the food. the doors at both ends close, and he can't get out!"

"I want the biggest trap!" Freddie stated. "I'm going to catch a great big animal!"

Dinah supplied meat for the bait, and Amos showed the children how to set the traps. Bert, Nan, and Harry carried theirs up into the woods. Flossie set hers by the house, but Freddie put his down near one of the cages.

"I wouldn't be able to carry my big animal far," he explained solemnly, "so he'll be handy to his new home."

The twins hated to leave, but Tom promised

to notify them if their traps caught anything.

The next day was Sunday. Harry and the twins drove into Meadowbrook with Aunt Sarah and Uncle Daniel to church. On the way home they stopped at the Holden farm.

"Have you looked at the traps this morning?" they called out to Tom, who welcomed them at the kitchen door.

"Only Freddie's and Flossie's. Nothing there yet. On the rest I was waiting for you," he replied with a grin.

Leaving Aunt Sarah and Uncle Daniel to talk to Dinah, the older children ran into the woods. Harry went with Bert to his trap.

"Something's in it!" cried Bert.

The animal had coarse grayish fur and a long rat-like tail.

"Say!" Harry exclaimed. "You've caught a nice 'possum!"

Bert looked at the motionless animal. "But he's dead!" he said sadly.

"No, he isn't!" Harry insisted. "He's just playing dead. Opossums always do that when they're frightened."

"Of course!" Bert looked relieved. "That's what we call 'playing possum.'"

Harry found a small red fox in his trap, while Nan had snared a fat rabbit.

"I believe this is Daddy Rabbit, who ran away!" cried Harry.

At this moment Flossie ran up breathlessly. "Come see what I caught!" she urged.

The older children carried their traps down to the cages and put the animals inside. Then they went to Flossie's trap. Inside a bushy squirrel was racing around, trying to find an opening so he could escape.

"He's terrible unhappy," said Flossie. "Tom, do you mind if I let him go?"

"I guess we'd better," Tom answered. "Squirrels aren't good in captivity. They gnaw at everything and usually end up escaping anyway." He let the little animal out, and it instantly ran up a tree.

The children now went to gather up the last trap—Freddie's. At first it appeared to be empty. Suddenly there was a little flutter at one end.

Tom whooped. "You caught a mouse, Freddie!"

The little boy looked as if he might burst into tears. "A great big trap, and all I got was a tiny mouse," he said sadly.

Nan hugged him. "Don't worry, Freddie!" she said. "I'm sure the mouse will be very interesting to tourists. Maybe it can learn some tricks."

Freddie cheered up a little, but he was still very quiet on the ride back to the Bobbsey farm. After they had eaten Martha's delicious din-

"You caught a mouse, Freddie!"

ner of fried chicken, the children gathered on the front porch with the Sunday paper.

They laughed at some of the comic strips. Then Bert turned to the local news. There was an article about the bank robberies which had taken place in the area.

"Listen to this!" Bert read aloud: "'It appears that in spite of efforts of local police, the state troopers, and the F.B.I., these criminals have remained free.'"

"And we haven't found them either!" Flossie said with a sigh.

"If we only had some idea of what they look like!" Nan added in a discouraged tone.

Bert turned a page of the newspaper. "Here's a funny one!" he cried. "A man has a white donkey to rent!"

Freddie ran up to look over Bert's shoulder. "Oh, boy—where, Bert?"

His brother pointed to the advertisement. "It's on Mr. Burns' farm. That's near here, isn't it, Harry?"

"Sure! Just down the road."

Freddie walked into the house, then ran up to the bedroom he shared with Bert. He reached into a drawer in the big, old-fashioned bureau and pulled out a little box.

"I haven't spent the money Daddy gave me when we left Lakeport," he thought. He dumped the contents of the box onto his bed.

There were several colorful stones which he had picked up at Boulder Lake, two tiny rubber fire engines, three dollar bills, and seven pennies.

Freddie's face fell. "I thought I had more money than this," he said to himself. Then he had an idea. "I'll see how much Flossie has!"

The little boy went to the top of the stairs and called down, "Flossie! Flossie!"

The front screen door banged as his twin ran into the house. "What, Freddie? Where are you?"

"Upstairs. Come here!"

Flossie clattered up the stairs. "What is it?"

"Nothing's the matter," Freddie replied. "I want some money. Do you have any?"

"You have money, Freddie," Flossie said. "Remember, Daddy gave us each some when he went away."

"I know," Freddie admitted, "but it isn't enough. I need two more dollars. Please give it to me."

"Well—all right." Flossie ran into her bedroom and returned with two crisp one dollar bills. "Now tell me why you want it."

"I *can't*," Freddie said. "It's a secret!"

CHAPTER XI

STRANGE BLACK STRIPES

"BUT Freddie!" Flossie wailed, "that's not fair! Tell me your secret about the money."

Freddie was already halfway down the stairs. He charged out the back door and down the lane. The children on the porch were busy with the newspaper and did not notice.

Farmer Burns was just coming out of the barn when Freddie raced into the barnyard. "Well! What's your hurry, young fellow?" the elderly man asked.

"I've come to rent your white donkey!" said Freddie breathlessly. "I have five real dollars!"

The farmer laughed. "Now just what do you want with a donkey?" he asked. "Aren't you Dan Bobbsey's nephew from Lakeport?"

Freddie explained about the disappearance of the animals from the Holden farm. "I'll give Tom the donkey to show to the tourists!"

Mr. Burns smiled. "Well, I'd certainly like to help out my neighbor. The donkey, Maria, is yours, but I never heard of anyone paying admission to see a donkey!" He turned and led a sleepy-looking white animal from the barn.

Freddie thanked the farmer and grasped the donkey's halter. As he walked slowly down the lane, he considered the man's remark. "Nobody would pay to see a donkey!"

"I told Tom I'd find him a big wild animal," Freddie thought, "and all I caught was that little mouse! And now this donkey is no good."

Freddie looked glum as he made his way back to Meadowbrook Farm. "I wish I had a real strange animal," he said to himself, "like a zebra!"

Then a thought came to him. He eyed the white donkey. "I could *make* a zebra out of her!" Freddie thought excitedly.

The little boy did not want the children on the front porch to see him with the donkey, so he left the road and cut through a field. This brought him to the Bobbsey barn out of the sight of Harry and the twins.

As Freddie crept into the barn leading the donkey, there was no one around. He tied Maria carefully to a post, then looked about him. He knew what he needed must be in the barn.

Freddie opened the door to a small storeroom in one corner of the big barn. On a shelf stood just what he wanted. A bucket of black paint! Nearby hung a collection of paint brushes.

Picking up the paint bucket and a brush, Freddie returned to the donkey. He opened the can and dipped the brush into the paint. Carefully he began to draw broad black stripes around the animal's front legs! When these were finished, he added stripes to the neck and forepart of the body.

Then Freddie dipped the brush in the sticky paint and stepped to the donkey's hind legs. At the first stroke of the brush, Maria lashed out with a vicious kick. Over went the bucket of black paint onto the barn floor!

"Now see what you've done!" Freddie scolded the donkey. He picked up the bucket. There was a small amount of paint left. As the little boy approached Maria with the brush, she kicked again.

Freddie backed away. He looked over his work. "I guess you'll just have to be half a zebra!" he finally said to the donkey.

With that he untied the rope and led Maria out of the barn and across the yard toward the house.

Bert was standing at the edge of the porch. He blinked in astonishment.

"Half a zebra!" Freddie said defiantly

"Freddie!" he cried, when he caught sight of his little brother and the strange-looking animal. "What on earth have you got there?"

"Half a zebra!" Freddie said defiantly. "I'm going to give him to Tom for his zoo!"

Nan, Flossie, and Harry jumped up and joined Bert to watch as Freddie coaxed the animal forward. The older children doubled over with laughter, but Flossie said stoutly, "I think he looks nice!"

At that moment Uncle Daniel came out of the house. He stood staring in disbelief, his hands on his hips.

"Freddie," he groaned, "what have you done to that poor animal?" But suddenly Uncle Daniel burst out laughing too.

"This is Maria. She's a zebra for the zoo!" Freddie replied.

His uncle became serious again. "I think you'd better get the paint off that animal, Freddie, before it dries."

"Yes, sir!" Freddie looked crestfallen as he turned toward the barn again.

Bert jumped off the porch and hurried after his little brother. "That was a good idea, Freddie," he said comfortingly, "but I don't think Maria is the kind of animal Tom wants."

Harry and the girls caught up with them. "We'll all help wash off the paint," Nan said.

The children found buckets which they filled with soap and water, and in a few minutes all five were scrubbing off the black stripes. The paint was still very wet, so it was easy to wash off.

"There!" said Bert with satisfaction. "That does it. I'll bet this donkey's never been so clean!"

When Maria was all white once more, Nan said, "Suppose Bert and I return the donkey to Mr. Burns."

"Sure!" her twin agreed.

"I'll stay here with Flossie," Freddie said, patting the confused animal. "Good-by, Maria." After a moment he added worriedly, "Bert, will you see if you can get Flossie's and my five dollars back?"

"Oh, sure."

When the donkey's owner saw Nan and Bert coming up his lane leading Maria, he looked surprised. "What's the matter?" he called. "Did she act up?"

Bert explained the situation, and Mr. Burns laughed. "Well, that's all right," he said. "No hard feelings!"

He put his hand into his pocket and pulled out the five one-dollar bills which Freddie had paid him. "You give these to the little fellow and tell him I'm sorry I didn't have a real zebra for him!"

The children thanked the farmer and hurried back to Meadowbrook.

That evening Uncle Daniel said he had a plan for the next day. "A friend of mine is thinking of starting barge rides for tourists on the old canal. He wants to know what I think of the idea. I told him I'd get a party of your friends together and take the trip tomorrow. What do you say?"

There was a chorus of 'yeas,' and Bert cried, "It sounds great!"

"What's a barge?" Flossie wanted to know.

Uncle Daniel told her that barges are flat-bottomed boats. "In olden days they were used to carry freight and passengers on the canals. They have no engines. The barges are pulled by mules who walk along the bank of the canal."

"We'll take a picnic lunch," Aunt Sarah said. "Call some of your friends, Harry, and see if they can go with us too."

In a few minutes Harry was back from the telephone with word that Patty, Kim, Tom, and Bud had accepted the invitation. They would meet near the canal where the barge was tied.

That night when the boys were getting ready for bed, Freddie said, "I don't know whether I can go on the canal or not. I want to find those robbers and win the money."

"This will be a good chance to look for them," Bert assured his brother. "A good detective looks for clues *wherever* he goes. Besides, Uncle Daniel says the canal runs through some back country, and the robbers could be hiding out there."

When Uncle Daniel drove up to the side of the house the next morning, Freddie was the first to climb into the station wagon. Flossie was close behind him.

"Who wants to skin the mules?" Uncle Daniel asked, when Aunt Sarah and the older children had joined them.

"Skin them!" Flossie looked horrified. "That's mean!"

The farmer laughed. "It's not so bad as it sounds!" he said. "A mule skinner is the person who drives or rides the mule!"

"Oh!" Flossie said, relieved. "That's diff-'rent!"

By this time they had reached the canal dock and joined the other boys and girls. The barge was tied to a post, and nearby two mules grazed quietly. The boat was low and flat with a platform at each end. Wooden seats ran around the sides.

After greetings had been exchanged, Aunt Sarah picked some blades of grass. "Why don't you draw lots for the first two children to ride the mules?" she suggested.

Bert and Nan drew the longest and shortest pieces of grass and were declared the winners. The mules were roped together, one behind the other, then that rope was fastened to one on the barge.

"Okay, Bert and Nan," Uncle Daniel called. "Your mules are named Peanuts and Popcorn. The lead mule is Peanuts."

"You take Peanuts, Bert," Nan said with a giggle. "I like Popcorn!"

The twins mounted the mules, and the others settled themselves on the wooden seats. Then with much creaking and groaning, the old barge edged out into the middle of the canal. Uncle Daniel sat on the platform at the rear, his hand guiding the large iron handle of the boat's rudder.

"Isn't it quiet?" Kim said as they glided along. There was no sound except that of the water lapping against the side of the barge and the *clop clop* of the mules' hoofs up ahead.

"Show us a little speed, Peanuts and Popcorn!" Harry called to the mules.

Bert and Nan obligingly dug their heels into the beasts' flanks, but the mules continued to plod along the worn path. There was not much for the riders to do but settle back to enjoy the scenery.

Several times Peanuts and Popcorn spotted an especially tempting bush and stopped to nibble the leaves. The rope connecting them to the barge would grow slack as the boat slipped toward them.

At one stop the path was very close to the water. "Come on, Peanuts!" Bert urged, slapping his mount on the flank.

With a toss of his head, Peanuts stopped munching and stepped smartly ahead. At this moment the rope running from Popcorn to the barge caught on a piece of iron pipe which stuck up from the bank. It looped around tightly and caused the mules to stop short. The barge still proceeded slowly ahead.

"I'll get the rope loose!" Nan called.

She leaned far down to release the rope, but could not reach it. As Nan started to sit up again, Popcorn twisted suddenly. Nan flew off the animal's back into the canal, right in the path of the moving barge!

CHAPTER XII

A LOG CABIN CLUE

FOR several seconds after her fall into the canal, Nan was too dazed to do anything more than sit up in the water. Then she saw the flat-bottomed boat bearing down upon her.

"Stop the boat!" Bert shouted from astride Peanuts. The mules were still held fast, but the barge continued to swing forward.

Desperately Uncle Daniel pulled the rudder to turn the clumsy vehicle away from Nan. But it responded slowly.

Splash! Harry had jumped into the shallow water of the canal near Nan. He seized her by one arm, pulled her to her feet, and dragged her out of the path of the boat. It glided past them.

"Oh, Harry," said Nan, "I was so scared, I couldn't move!"

By this time the barge had lost momentum

and stopped. Everyone clambered to the side of the boat and helped Nan and Harry aboard.

"Are you all right?" Aunt Sarah asked the two anxiously. When Nan and Harry had assured her that they were, Aunt Sarah told them to sit on the low platform at the bow of the barge.

"You'll be in the sun there and get dry quickly," she told them.

"It's time for someone else to skin the mules!" Bert said with a grin as he slid off Peanuts.

Tom and Kim were chosen. They took their places on Peanuts and Popcorn. Bert unwound the rope and the barge trip resumed.

A short time later, Freddie and Flossie began to grow restless and started playing tag around the deck. But even this did not hold their interest for long. Nan had been watching and finally spoke up. "How about a new game?" she asked.

"Sure!" Bert agreed. "What'll it be?"

"We might play 'Whisper Down the Lane,'" Patty suggested.

Flossie looked puzzled. "How can we do that if we're on a barge?"

Everyone laughed. "That's a good question," Patty said with a grin. She then explained that the players sat in a circle. The first one whispered a message into the ear of the person seated next to her. Then that person passed on the message by whispering to the player on the other side of her.

"Lots of times the last message is a lot different from the first one," Patty concluded.

"That sounds like fun," Nan remarked. "Shall I start?"

The children formed a circle on the deck. At Patty's nod, Nan leaned toward Harry and rapidly whispered a message into his ear.

Quickly Harry turned and told it to Patty. The girl laughed as she passed the message to Freddie.

The little boy looked puzzled, but put his lips to Bud's ear and said something. He in turn whispered it to Bert. Flossie was the last.

"What's the message?" Nan asked impatiently.

Flossie giggled. "It's silly, but it sounded like 'Who put the pin in the itching cake?' "

Everyone roared with laughter. Then Patty asked, "What did you really say, Nan?"

"My message was, 'Who will win the homing pigeon race?' " Nan replied.

After a few moments of discussion over just *who* had changed the message, Nan turned to Harry. "Now you start one," she urged.

Harry thought a minute, then whispered to

Patty. The message was passed around the circle of children. Nan was the last this time.

"What did you start, Harry?" she asked with a chuckle. "What I got was, 'Bert is a mud shrimp and he runs pumps!' "

Harry burst out laughing. "What I really said was, 'Bert is a mule skinner when he rides Peanuts!' "

Everyone noticed that Bert was not laughing. Instead, he was looking intently toward the shore. At this point the canal ran through a strip of woods.

"Uncle Daniel!" Bert called. "Can we stop a minute?"

"Sure! What's the matter?" his uncle asked, giving a blast on a whistle he carried. At the signal the mules stopped.

"I saw a man dart behind some trees over there," Bert explained. "I'd like to go after him and see why he's hiding."

"You think he's one of the robbers?" Bud asked.

"He could be."

"Bud, you go with Bert," said Uncle Daniel.

The two boys jumped to the bank and disappeared among the trees. Bert held up his hand for silence. As he and Bud listened, they heard someone running through the underbrush.

"It's this way!" Bert whispered.

The two boys dashed through the woods. Ahead they could spot the dark figure of a man dodging in and out among the trees. But they could not get near enough to see what he looked like.

Suddenly Bud caught his foot on a tree root and pitched headlong. Bert stopped to help him up. By this time the man was out of sight.

"We've lost him!" Bud exclaimed in disappointment. "And it's all my fault!"

"Never mind," Bert consoled him. "I don't think we could have caught him anyhow. But let's search for clues. Maybe we can find out why the man was in the woods."

Bud stopped and looked around. "You know," he said slowly, "I think I've been in these woods before. We're not very far from the Holden farm."

A moment later he went on, "There used to be an old log cabin somewhere in here. Maybe that man is living in it."

"A cabin!" Bert cried. "Show me where it is!"

"I don't know whether or not I can," Bud replied doubtfully. "I haven't been here for a long time."

The boys walked on through the woods looking from side to side. There was no sign of a log cabin. Just as they were about to give up, Bert said excitedly, "There it is!"

Ahead was a clearing. At one side of it stood a small log cabin. As the boys approached, they could see that it was in bad condition. The door hung on one hinge, the roof had a big hole in it, and the glass had been knocked out of the windows.

"I'm sure the man's not living here now!" Bud said in disappointment. "The place is falling down!"

"Let's look around," Bert suggested. He walked to the door and peered inside.

There was no furniture in the room, and the floor was covered with dead leaves and dust. It looked as if no one had entered the place for some time.

"I guess there aren't any clues here!"

Bert turned away and walked around to the back of the little building. Here the ground was damp, and Bert noticed two footprints at the edge of a wooded path. He bent to examine them.

"Bud!" he called. "Look at these prints! They're like the ones we saw on our camping trip. One is real narrow!"

"The camping spot and this one aren't far apart," Bud remarked. "The mountain is just on the other side of these woods."

"Of course, these prints could have been made by some innocent person," Bert admitted.

"Bud!" he called. "Look at these prints!"

"But if they were, why did that man run away?"

"I wish we knew what those bank robbers look like," said Bud. "Then it would be easier to find them!"

"I wonder," said Bert, "if the police have found out yet. I'm going to ask them."

"Maybe we'd better get back to the barge," Bud suggested. "We've been gone quite a while."

With Bud taking the lead, the two boys made their way back. When they reached the water, the barge was not there!

"I guess we're farther down the canal than where we got off the barge," Bud ventured.

"I remember there was a tall pine tree on the opposite bank where we stopped," Bert said. "That looks like it up there."

The boys made their way along the towpath and soon came in sight of the anchored barge.

Nan saw them coming. "Any luck?" she called.

"No. The man got away," Bert replied.

"You're just in time for the picnic," said Flossie. "We're opening the baskets!"

By the time the boys jumped aboard, a delicious-looking lunch had been spread on the platform in the bow. The children were hungry and soon were munching the fried chicken which Martha had put into the picnic hampers.

Bert and Bud told about finding the deserted cabin and the familiar-looking footprints. The other children were excited. Freddie was positive they belonged to the robbers.

When the picnic food was gone, the girls packed the refuse back into the basket. Uncle Daniel pulled the big iron rudder handle out of its hole in the platform and carried it to the other end of the barge. The children looked puzzled.

"It's sure an easy way to turn around!" he said as he fitted the handle into another hole.

Bud Stout and Patty Manners jumped ashore and climbed up onto the mules' backs. When the animals had been turned, and the rope fastened, the barge began its homeward journey.

When the picnickers reached the dock, Bud Stout's brother was there in his green car. After many thanks to Mr. Bobbsey, Bud, Tom, Kim, and Patty drove away with him. The Bobbsey twins and Harry piled into the station wagon and Uncle Daniel headed for Meadowbrook Farm.

A few minutes later Harry observed, "That car coming toward us is sure speeding."

"Looks like a state trooper!" Uncle Daniel remarked. "He must be answering an alarm!"

Soon the car sped by. But when the driver saw the Bobbseys, he slammed on his brakes.

"Dad!" Harry cried. "He wants to talk to us."

Uncle Daniel stopped the station wagon. At the same time, the policeman backed up until he was even with the other car.

"Mr. Bobbsey!" he called. "The bank in Rosedale has just been robbed!"

CHAPTER XIII

THE PUZZLING CAPSULE

ANOTHER bank robbery! The children looked at one another in dismay.

Bert wanted to question the trooper, but the policeman sped away. As soon as Uncle Daniel reached the farm, Bert dashed to the telephone and called headquarters. He asked for a description of the men.

"We have a very general description of the holdup men at Rosedale," the lieutenant said. "One of them was stocky while the other was quite thin. They got away in a green car, so we assume it's the same two who have robbed the other banks. The narrow footprints you saw could belong to one of the men."

Bert wanted to do more sleuthing and told his twin.

"I do too," Nan said. "Let's walk over to

Tom's house to see how our animals are getting along. On the way we can look for the green car, and the men."

All the children walked there. Dinah was delighted when they came into the Holden kitchen. "Well now, isn't this surprisin'?" she said with a chuckle. "I was just goin' to make some fudge. Can you stay and have some?"

"Freddie and I will help you!" Flossie cried. The small twins loved to be with Dinah in the kitchen and often helped her when they were at home in Lakeport.

At this moment Tom came into the room. "Hi!" he said. "I thought I heard your voices. Come see the animals."

Freddie and Flossie could not resist going with the others for a look.

"I miss the bears!" Tom commented sadly. "Dad had taught them so many tricks, they were fun to watch."

The children walked around and gazed at the other animals. The fox and opossum seemed to be doing well. Amos Berg had found a baby fawn in some bushes that morning, and had added it to the animal farm.

"Let's go down to the back road by the woods," Bert suggested, after they had seen all the animals. "The thieves may have left the green car again."

"Remember, Freddie," Flossie said, "we're going to help Dinah."

Freddie hesitated. He was torn between the desire to be a detective and his love for candy. His desire for sweets won out.

"Okay," he said, and followed Flossie toward the house.

The older children trekked down the lane, across the highway, and into a field. At the end of it, they came to the rutted country road.

Bert walked along it for a short distance, looking carefully at the ground. It was dry, and the deep ruts showed no sign that a car had been driven through them recently.

"No luck here!" Bert said in a discouraged tone.

"How about showing us the log cabin you found this morning?" Harry asked eagerly. "Maybe we could camp out in it some time."

"I'll try to find it," Bert agreed. "But I wish Bud were here. He knows his way around these woods better than I do!"

"I'd like to help," Tom said, "but I've never seen the cabin. I didn't even know there was one in there."

The four children left the road and entered the woods. It was cool and shady.

"Which direction is the canal?" Bert asked Tom.

His friend pointed to the left.

"Let's go that way." Bert turned left and began to pick his way through the underbrush. The others followed.

In a little while they found a path which wound among the trees. It led them deeper and deeper into the forest.

"Are you sure you're going the right way?" Nan asked in a worried tone.

"I think so," her brother replied. "I remember noticing a stream near the cabin, so I thought this was probably the same one." He pointed to a little brook which gurgled along beside the path.

The children walked in silence for a time. Then Bert stopped. "The path branches here," he said. "I'm not sure which way to go."

"Let's try the right-hand one," Harry proposed. "It looks a little better."

Five minutes later Bert stopped again. "You were right, Harry!" he cried. "There's the cabin!"

Nan and the boys ran forward. "Say, this is neat!" Harry said admiringly. "We could use it for a camp!"

Tom pushed his way around the sagging door. Bert and Harry followed him into the one-room cabin. The boys eagerly began to plan how they could fix it up.

Nan wandered around outside. Suddenly she saw a bit of metal gleaming in the sunlight which drifted through the trees. Idly she bent down and picked it up.

It was an aluminum capsule about three-quarters of an inch long, fastened to a sort of clamp.

"I wonder what it's used for?" Nan thought, examining it more closely.

At that moment the boys came out of the cabin.

"Look what I found!" Nan called to them.

Bert stared at the capsule. "What is it?" he asked curiously.

Tom reached out and took it from Bert's hand. "This is a pigeon message capsule!"

"What's a message capsule?" Nan inquired.

Harry explained that a pigeon, when carrying a message, has the tiny capsule clamped onto one leg. "The message is folded up very small and stuffed into this container," he said.

"Is there anything in this one?" Nan asked excitedly.

Tom pulled the capsule apart. It was empty!

"Oh!" Nan sighed in disappointment. "I thought I had found a good clue!"

"Maybe you have!" Bert said. "How did that pigeon capsule get here?"

No one could answer the question. Still puzzling over it, Bert slipped the aluminum container into his pocket. Then the children started back to the farmhouse.

This time the way seemed easy to find. They walked briskly along the path, laughing and talking as they went.

Tom was ahead. Suddenly he stopped. "There's something moving in those bushes," he said to Bert, who was directly behind him.

Nan and Harry stopped talking and looked questioningly at the two boys. Tom put a finger to his lips and crept stealthily forward. The others waited.

Then there came a particularly loud rustling and a bear cub stepped out into the path! He shuffled toward the children, his head weaving from side to side.

"Run!" Nan cried as she turned to retreat. Bert and Harry started to follow.

"Wait!" Tom called out. To the amazement of the other children, he walked toward the bear and began to whistle a tune.

"Tom!" Harry yelled. "You're crazy! That bear will attack you!"

But Tom continued to whistle as he approached the bear. All at once the cub stood up on his hind legs and began a clumsy shuffle in a small circle.

"He's dancing!" Bert cried.

"He's dancing!" Bert cried

"It's Arthur!" Nan exclaimed at the same time.

Tom turned around, triumphant. "I thought it was Arthur, but I wasn't sure until he began to dance."

The four children gathered around the bear. A frayed bit of rope dangled from his collar.

"He must have been tied up somewhere and broke loose," Harry said.

Nan took hold of the collar and began to lead the cub along the path. "He's been hurt!" she cried. "He's limping!"

Tom bent down to examine Arthur's leg. "He has a bad cut. Let's get him home, and Amos will fix him up!"

As Nan, the boys, and Arthur walked along the lane to the Holden farmhouse, Freddie and Flossie ran out the kitchen door.

"It's Arthur!" Flossie shouted, and began to jump up and down.

"Where did you find him?" Freddie asked, his eyes wide with amazement.

Tom turned the bear cub over to Amos, and the children trooped into the kitchen. There, between big bites of creamy fudge, they told the small twins and Dinah about capturing Arthur.

"Well, I declare!" Dinah cried. "If you all haven't had a day!"

Soon afterward the Bobbseys left. At home

Freddie and Flossie said it was suppertime for Snoop and went in search of their cat. They found him asleep under a bush.

"Come, Snoopie!" Freddie urged, tickling the cat under his chin.

At that moment Aunt Sarah called from the back porch, "Freddie! Flossie! Would you like to feed the turkeys for me?"

"Oh, yes!" Flossie agreed, jumping up and hurrying to her aunt. Freddie followed her, holding Snoop.

"Just sprinkle this grain around the turkey run," Aunt Sarah directed, handing the twins a full pail.

The turkeys came running when they saw the two children arriving with the feed. *"Gobble! Gobble!"* Snoop jumped from Freddie's arms and stood watching.

For a while the work went well. Freddie and Flossie scattered the grain, and the turkeys gobbled it up.

"Don't grab!" Flossie cried when one big bird stuck his long neck into her pail.

"Come back here!" Freddie shouted to another turkey, who ran toward the fence.

Snoop pricked up his ears. He crouched, then began to creep along the ground toward the runaway turkey. The next minute he broke into a gallop.

The turkey gave a loud squawk and raced

across the yard with Snoop in close pursuit. Suddenly the turkey turned. With a great flapping of wings, it rose into the air, then swooped down directly on the cat.

Snoop let out an anguished yowl. The turkey had the cat's tail firmly held in its beak!

CHAPTER XIV

A WARNING NOTE

"HELP!" Flossie screamed when she saw what was happening to Snoop. "Somebody come and save our cat!"

"I will!" Freddie shouted. He dropped the feed bucket and dashed to a hose attached to a faucet on the barn.

Ssss! The water streamed out of the hose onto the turkey's head. The big bird paid no attention, and Snoop's yowls grew louder.

"Oh! Oh!" Flossie wailed.

Suddenly the stream of cold water hit the turkey in one eye. Abruptly the bird let go of the cat's tail! Snoop climbed the fence, raced across the yard, and into the kitchen!

"Freddie, you're a real hero!" Flossie cried.

At supper that evening Harry reminded his cousins that the Meadowbrook Pigeon Club race was to take place the next day.

"Nan and Bert, are you still going to help Tom and me?" he asked the twins.

Nan replied that she would be at the Holden loft to clock in Tom's birds. "And I'll be here to welcome your winner!" Bert added.

"But I want to see the pigeons start to race!" Flossie protested.

"I do too!" Freddie piped up.

"All right," said Harry.

It was decided that Freddie and Flossie would ride into Meadowbrook with him. They would meet Tom at the starting point.

The next morning after Nan had left for the Holden farm, the small twins climbed into the rear of the station wagon. Harry got in the front seat with his father, who would drive them to town.

"I think I'll put the pigeons on the middle seat," he said a moment later.

Harry picked up the wicker basket and lifted it over the back of the front seat. As he did, the basket hit against the side of the car and the catch came open. The next instant the air seemed to be full of pigeons!

"Close the windows!" Harry yelled as he desperately struggled to grab one of the birds flapping over his head.

Quickly Freddie and Flossie rolled up the rear window while Uncle Daniel closed his.

Harry wound up the other window.

"I caught a pigeon!" Freddie cried. He had reached up and put his hands around a bird which had settled on the back of the center seat.

Harry had managed to catch the other bird before it escaped.

"Wow! That was a close call!" Harry gasped. He put the two pigeons back into the basket and made sure that the latch was secure. "I hope they didn't hurt their wings," he added anxiously as Uncle Daniel started the car.

"One of them lost a feather!" Flossie said, holding up a long white one. "Can he fly all right without it?"

Harry assured her that the loss of one feather would not hurt the bird. "Maybe he'll go even faster now!" he added.

A little later they drove up to the small park in the center of the town of Meadowbrook. A crowd had already gathered. There were four other contestants besides Harry and Tom. They all stood in a group near the starting point. Each carried his pigeons in a wicker basket.

Tom ran up to greet Harry and the small twins. "You're late!" he said. "I was afraid you weren't coming!"

Harry told him about their adventure before leaving the farm. Tom laughed. "Maybe your

birds are tired now, and mine will beat them!"
he teased.

Mr. Grimes, the starter, called the contestants together. He held up a broad band of rubber. "As you all know, we'll put one of these on a leg of each pigeon. When the pigeon arrives at his home loft, the attendant there will remove it. Then he'll place it in the pigeon timer machine which you all have. This records the exact time the bird arrives."

"How soon will we know who wins?" Flossie asked.

"Come back here at four o'clock this afternoon," Mr. Grimes replied. "We'll announce the winner then."

While he had been talking, another man had been slipping the rubber markers on the pigeons.

"When I blow my whistle," Mr. Grimes instructed, "open the sides of the baskets."

A moment later he gave the signal. The doors were opened and the pigeons flew out.

"They're off!" Freddie shouted, and Flossie jumped up and down in excitement.

Most of the birds rose into the air, then quickly moved off in the direction of their lofts. But one of Harry's pigeons flew around in circles just above the small twins' heads.

"Whistle and clap your hands!" Harry di-

"Whistle and clap your hands!" Harry directed frantically

rected frantically. "We must get him started!"

Freddie put two fingers between his teeth and blew a shrill blast. Flossie clapped her hands as hard as she could. Finally the pigeon stopped circling and headed off in the direction of the farm.

At the Holdens' loft, Nan waited tensely for the return of Tom's two pigeons. When she saw them flying toward her, she glanced quickly at the clock on the shelf. It seemed to her that they had made very good time.

"I hope Tom wins," she said to herself. "He felt so bad when his animals were stolen, this may cheer him up."

The two pigeons came in through the trap door a moment later. Nan took off the rubber bands and put them in the time clock. Next she gave the birds food and water. Before leaving the farm, Nan stopped in to say hello to Dinah.

The cook handed her a box. "A few of Dinah's cookies," she said, with a wide grin.

"Oh, thanks, Dinah. They won't last long when I show them to the twins and Harry!"

Nan hurried home and asked if her cousin's pigeons had made good time.

Bert shook his head sadly. "One came in very soon, but the second bird isn't here yet!"

"Isn't here!" Nan repeated in astonishment.

"What do you suppose happened to it?"

Bert shrugged. "I don't know. Harry says the birds are sometimes blown off course."

"But there's no wind today!" Nan protested.

At that moment the station wagon turned into the lane. Bert ran forward to tell his cousin about the missing bird.

Harry looked disturbed. "Now I have only one entry!" he cried. "I don't stand much chance of winning!"

After the noon dinner Uncle Daniel said he had some business in town. He would take the time clocks from Tom's and Harry's lofts to the Pigeon Club headquarters.

"I'll see you in the park at four o'clock," he promised as he drove away.

"I want to start training some of my young pigeons," Harry said. "Anyone want to help?"

"Sure," replied Bert. "I think we all would!"

The children went out to the loft which, like Tom's, was built on an extension of the roof.

"What are you going to do?" Nan asked with interest.

Harry pointed to several birds roosting on a series of wooden slats. "Those pigeons are a month old now," he said. "It's time for their training to begin."

Harry shooed them from their perches, and with whistles and waving of arms kept them flying about the loft. "This strengthens their wings," he explained.

"What can I do?" Bert wanted to know.

"You can take a couple of birds and show them how to come through the trap doors," his cousin suggested.

"I'll help," Nan volunteered.

The twins set the pigeons on the landing platform, then opened the doors and pushed the birds in. After several minutes the pigeons learned to open the traps themselves.

"Now let's try a couple of short flights," Harry proposed.

"Freddie and I want to do something!" Flossie insisted.

"Okay." Harry picked up two birds and handed them to the small twins. "These pigeons haven't had anything to eat today. Take them as far as the house, then let them loose. They'll fly here for food. In the meantime I'll feed the other birds. Their pecking noises and fluttering should make these two babies fly back to the loft."

Feeling very important, Freddie and Flossie walked toward the house with the pigeons clutched tightly in their arms.

Bert and Nan helped fill the feeders, and soon the pigeons were eating noisily. Suddenly there was a whir of wings. One baby bird, then another, came in through the traps.

"Flossie and Freddie did a good job," said Bert.

"A third bird just came in!" Nan exclaimed. "I thought Freddie and Flossie took only two!"

"They did!" Harry ran over and picked up the third pigeon. "This is my other racing entry!"

"Look! There's a capsule on his leg!" Bert cried in surprise.

"But I didn't put one on him!" Harry said, looking bewildered.

Freddie and Flossie came back into the loft. "Open it. Quick!" Flossie urged, when the older children explained about the return of the missing pigeon.

Harry carefully took the capsule from the bird's leg and opened it. There was a piece of paper inside.

"Let me take it out!" Freddie begged.

His cousin handed him the tiny container, and Freddie pulled out the paper. He unfolded it carefully and handed it back. "There's writing on it. Read it!" he urged.

Harry scanned the short message, then read aloud:

"'Keep your pigeons out of the woods. And stay out yourself! Danger!'"

CHAPTER XV

HAYMOW DETECTIVES

DANGER! The children looked at one another in bewilderment.

"Where did the pigeon get the note?" Flossie asked. "Who put it on him?"

"That's another mystery to solve!" Bert told her.

"I can't understand," said Harry, "how anyone could get hold of my pigeon."

Nan looked worried. "Who do you suppose wants to keep us out of the woods?" she asked. "Do you think it's the bank robbers, and they're hiding in there?"

"They could be," Harry admitted.

Suddenly Nan thought of something. "Remember, I found a message capsule near that cabin in the woods?" she reminded the boys.

"But no one was there," Bert argued, "and anyway, why would Harry's pigeon come down there?"

"Sometimes," said Harry excitedly, "a homing pigeon stops at another pigeon loft."

"But there was no sign of a loft around the cabin!" Nan told him.

"Let's have another look at that cabin," Bert suggested eagerly.

Flossie shivered. "Ooh! I'd be scared to go into the woods now!"

"I don't think we should go there again without a policeman," Nan spoke up.

At that moment there came a call from the yard. "Children! It's time to start for town and find out who won the pigeon race."

"That's Mother," Harry said. "We'd better get Rocket ready if we're going to drive the pony cart to Meadowbrook."

It did not take long to harness the little Shetland, and soon the children were rolling along the road to town. When they reached the park, Mr. Grimes was already there. A crowd of other contestants and their friends was gathered around him.

"Who won the race?" Flossie asked as she ran up to the man.

"I'll tell you in a minute," said Mr. Grimes. He looked over the crowd, then picked up a loudspeaker.

"Ladies and gentlemen," he said, "it gives me great pleasure to announce that the winner of the first race of the Meadowbrook Pigeon Club is—" He paused and smiled.

"Oh, please tell us!" Flossie jumped up and down in excitement.

Mr. Grimes gave the little girl a broad wink. "The winner is Harry Bobbsey of Meadowbrook Farm," he cried.

"Goody! Goody!" Flossie burst out. "Harry won!"

There was loud applause. The twins slapped their cousin on the back.

"And now," Mr. Grimes went on, "if Harry will come forward, we will give him his prize!"

Beaming with happiness, Harry walked up. Mr. Grimes handed him a silver cup. "Your name will be engraved on this trophy," he explained. "You may keep it until next year's race."

Harry thanked Mr. Grimes and passed the cup around among the other contestants to be admired.

"I hope my name will be on there some day!" Tom said with a chuckle.

"I'll be rooting for you next year," Harry assured his friend.

"Don't they give a prize to the pigeon, too?" Freddie asked curiously.

Harry grinned at the little boy. "I'll give

him some extra seeds for supper. Okay?"

Freddie nodded happily.

As the Bobbseys started home, Nan said, "Let's take the back way. I know it's farther, but it's so much prettier."

"Okay," said Bert, who was driving.

Outside of town he turned the pony down a little-used road which wound through the countryside. Rocket trotted along briskly in the late afternoon sunshine.

"I'm glad your pigeon won the race, Harry," Nan remarked, "but I'm sorry Tom couldn't win too!"

"Well—" Harry started to reply, but at that moment Rocket shied violently. Harry clutched the side of the basket cart to keep from pitching out. It was all Bert could do to bring the pony to a halt.

"What's the matter?" Nan asked in astonishment.

"There was something shiny in those bushes back there," Bert explained. "I guess it scared Rocket!"

"Let's see what it was!" Harry jumped out of the cart and walked back up the road. When he pushed aside the bushes, he called excitedly to the others.

"Come here! Look what I've found!"

The twins scrambled out of the pony cart

There, almost entirely hidden, was an old green car

and ran back to Harry. *There, almost entirely hidden by the bushes, was an old green car!*

"The bank robbers' car!" Bert exclaimed. "The metal door handle must have caught the light and made Rocket shy!"

"Do you think the robbers are around here?" Flossie glanced nervously over her shoulder.

"I don't know," Nan replied, "but we ought to get word to the state troopers about the car right away! We're not far from the Holden farm. Let's drive up there and phone them."

"Okay," Bert agreed.

The call was made, and in a short time Lieutenant Kent and Officer Bennett drove up. The lieutenant said they would follow the pony cart to the spot where the green car was hidden.

When Bert reached it, he stopped. All the children got out and showed the troopers what they had seen concealed in the woods. They waited excitedly while Lieutenant Kent took a notebook from his pocket to look up the description of the bank robbers' car. He compared it with the car before him.

"This is the car we've been looking for, all right!" he said. "Good work, children!"

"Rocket's really the one who found it!" Freddie said proudly.

The two troopers examined the car and the

ground around it, but found no further clue to the robbers.

"Let's see if there's anything in the trunk," Trooper Bennett suggested. The rear compartment was locked, but it did not take the policemen long to break it open.

Lieutenant Kent lifted the top. "Nothing in here," he said in disappointment. "Just a spare tire and a bag of grain!"

"Grain!" Harry cried. "What kind?"

He stuck his hand into the bag and pulled out a handful of the seeds. "This looks like pigeon feed!" he exclaimed.

"Pigeon feed!" Nan repeated. She turned to the troopers. "We think maybe the bank robbers have a pigeon loft somewhere in the woods." She told about the warning note on Harry's pigeon.

Officer Kent frowned, then went to his car radio to report to his chief. He received a startling answer.

"A good tip came in a short time ago that the men we're after have just robbed another bank some distance from here. They headed in a direction away from this one," he told the children.

"Goody! Goody!" said Flossie.

Freddie added, "Now we can go in the woods all we want to!"

Lieutenant Kent took a chain from his car. "We'll tow this green car into headquarters for evidence," he said.

When the troopers started off with the old automobile, the children waved, then headed for home. Aunt Sarah and Uncle Daniel listened in astonishment to the children's latest adventure.

"What will you do next, you young detectives?" Aunt Sarah said.

After supper Harry called Bert aside. "I'm worried," he said. "Maybe the same men did rob another bank today and aren't coming back here. But they might have a friend in the woods with pigeons."

"That's right," Bert agreed. "But what of it?"

"The man might come and steal my prize pigeon!" Harry answered. "Bert, are you game to sleep out in the haymow with me so we can grab anybody who comes to the pigeon loft?"

"Sure," said Bert.

"Let's keep it a secret from everyone but Mother and Dad," Harry suggested.

The boys received permission and agreed to sneak out to the barn when the other children were asleep.

Later that night Harry crept into the room which Bert shared with Freddie. "Sst!" He hissed. "Ready?"

Bert jumped out of bed and pulled on his jeans over his pajamas. He and Harry were just leaving the room when suddenly Freddie's voice piped up. "Where are you going?"

"You need your sleep, Freddie," said Bert. "Close your eyes."

Instead, Freddie sat up and leaned on his elbow. "I want to come too!" he insisted, jumping out of bed.

Bert looked at Harry, who nodded. "All right," he said. "Put on some clothes. We're going to sleep in the hay and listen for anybody who bothers the pigeons."

When Freddie was ready, the three boys went quietly downstairs. They could hear Uncle Daniel and Aunt Sarah talking on the porch. As the boys crept through the kitchen, Bert saw a bag of pigeon feed on a table. He filled one of his pockets with the grain.

"I might need it," he said, "in case we have to rescue a pigeon."

The cousins ran silently across the yard and into the barn. A few minutes later they were snuggling down into the sweet-smelling hay.

"I'm not sleepy any more," Freddie said. "Tell me a story, Bert!"

"How about a ghost story?" Harry proposed. "I know some great ones!"

"Okay," Bert agreed. "You start."

Harry told a story which was full of strange sounds, eerie lights, and loud shrieks. By the time he finished, Freddie was shivering.

"Think you can stand another one?" Bert asked him teasingly.

"Sure!" Freddie insisted. "I'm brave!"

Bert's tale was about a haunted house where doors slammed when no one was near them, and lights turned themselves on mysteriously. He was just reaching the end, when a man's deep voice came up to them from the barnyard.

At the same moment Freddie pointed a shaky finger toward the corner of the haymow. Two large eyes were watching them intently!

CHAPTER XVI

A FUNNY CODE

"WH—who is it?" Freddie quavered.

"I don't know," Bert whispered. He was about to challenge the stranger when the voice they had heard before sounded again. This time it came from the barn below them!

Freddie gasped. "L-let's get out of here!" he said. "I'm scared!"

The boys were scrambling to their feet when a head appeared over the edge of the haymow. "Is Freddie up there?" a voice inquired. It was Uncle Daniel's!

"Yes, Dad, he's here," Harry replied.

At that moment a big bird flew past them and out the window. Then they heard a *whooo* from a nearby tree.

Harry burst out laughing. "Those eyes we saw belong to an owl, fellows!"

Bert and Freddie joined in the laughter. "I wasn't really scared except for a minute," Freddie insisted.

"You should have told us you were taking Freddie," said Uncle Daniel. "Come back to the house, all of you. Aunt Sarah and I were really worried when we found Freddie gone."

Sheepishly the three boys descended the ladder.

"We're sorry," said Bert.

"How can we guard the pigeons if we're not here?" Harry asked.

"I'm sure the birds will be all right," his father said, "and you boys will be much more comfortable in your beds."

The three followed him quietly across the yard and soon were asleep in their own rooms.

The next morning at breakfast Uncle Daniel had a good time teasing the boys about their escapade of the night before. "And to think that you, Harry, raised on a farm, were afraid of an owl!" he added with a laugh.

Harry grinned. "I guess it was Bert's ghost story that really scared me!"

Later Freddie and Flossie went off to play in the orchard with Snoop. Nan wandered out to the kitchen and soon was helping Aunt Sarah and Martha make apple butter.

"How about working with the pigeons?" Harry proposed to Bert. "I'd like to take two of the young ones for a practice flight."

"Neat idea." The two boys started out with

two pigeons in a wicker basket. They walked to a field which bordered the Holden farm.

"This is the farthest I've tried to send these birds," Harry said, "but their cote mates are back in the loft, so that should bring them home."

By this time the cousins had reached the field. Harry selected a spot where the ground rose slightly and put down the basket.

"I won't be able to time them," he remarked, "because there's no one at the loft to clock them in. But at least I can see if they fly home."

Harry and Bert flopped down on the ground, and Harry prepared to open the basket. Just then a strange pigeon alighted on top of the wicker container!

"Where did he come from?" Bert asked in amazement. "Is he one of yours, Harry?"

His cousin shook his head. He picked up the pigeon carefully. "No. See, he doesn't have a registration band."

"But look!" Bert exclaimed. "He has a capsule on his leg!"

"That's queer," Harry remarked. "He seems to be a carrier pigeon, yet he hasn't been registered."

Harry examined the bird. "His wing is injured. I guess the poor little guy couldn't fly any farther."

"Let's open the capsule and see if there's a message in it!" Bert proposed eagerly.

"All right," his cousin agreed. "The pigeon can't deliver it, so maybe we can help if we read the message."

He detached the tiny cylinder from the bird's leg, and Bert opened it. "There *is* a message!" Bert cried. He was so excited that he had difficulty in pulling the tightly folded paper from the container.

"Hurry! Let me see it!" Harry urged.

Bert spread out the paper on top of the basket. Printed in black letters were the words:

Every girl raves about boys

"It's just a joke!" Harry exclaimed in disappointment.

"But why would anyone play a joke like that?" Bert asked in bewilderment. He was quiet for a while, then he said slowly, "You know, it may *not* be a joke. It could be a message in code—from the bank robbers!"

"But they've left here," said Harry.

"Maybe they're back, Harry. And don't forget, they may have a friend here who has their pigeons."

"Okay," said Harry. "If the message is from the robbers, what does it mean? It sounds pretty silly to me!"

Bert studied the paper from all angles. He held it up towards the sun and peered at it.

"There doesn't seem to be anything unusual about the paper," he decided. "I'm sure the words make up some sort of code message."

The two boys pored over the writing for a while, but were not able to decipher its meaning. Finally Harry gave up. "You go on trying if you want to," he said. "I think I'll send my pigeons on their way home."

"Okay," Bert agreed. Then he had an idea. "Wait a minute, Harry! Remember, we were going to look around that cabin again? Let's do it now!"

Harry paused in the act of opening the basket. "I know something else we could do! We could put the capsule on one of my pigeons and send it home!"

"Great! And we can put a note on your other pigeon explaining about the message and asking Nan to work on it. We'll tell her we'll be home after we've looked around the cabin again!"

Harry had a sudden thought. "But what if she doesn't go to the cote to see the messages?"

"We'll just have to hope she does," Bert said encouragingly. He hunted in his pockets and found a small notebook and a stub of pencil. The boys composed their message. Then they wound the paper around one of the bird's legs and secured it with a rubber band.

Harry fastened the capsule to the leg of the other pigeon. Finally he tossed both birds into the air. They fluttered their wings for a moment, then flew off in the direction of Meadowbrook Farm.

"What shall we do about this injured bird?" Bert asked.

"I'll take him along and fix his wing when we get home," Harry replied, putting the bird into the wicker basket.

The boys walked across the field and entered the woods. They made their way through the underbrush until they came to a narrow path.

"Is this the way to the cabin?" Bert asked, pausing uncertainly.

"I think so," Harry replied. "At least we're going in the right direction."

They trudged along in silence for a few minutes. The path became narrower. Then, just when the boys had decided they were lost, it joined another path.

"I'm sure this is right," Bert said in a relieved tone. "This looks like the same path Bud and I found that first day."

Another ten minutes' hike brought them to a clearing. There was the cabin, looking just as deserted as when Bert had first come upon it.

Bert and Harry ran to the door and looked in. The floor was still covered with dirt and dead leaves.

"I'm sure no one has been in here," Harry said.

"I guess you're right." Bert sounded disappointed.

Harry set the pigeon basket down on the ground. The bird inside stirred restlessly.

"But where did that pigeon come from?" Bert demanded. "Let's scout around in the woods near here. Maybe we can find a clue!"

The two boys walked around the clearing in an ever widening circle. In a few minutes, they were out of sight of the cabin. Suddenly the injured pigeon began fluttering its wings and making a cooing noise.

"I think there are other pigeons near here!" Harry declared excitedly. "Listen!"

The cousins stood still, straining their ears. A faint fluttering sound came from their left. They walked in that direction.

"There's something under those branches there!" Bert whispered. He crept toward the spot. Harry followed.

The next instant both boys were seized from behind!

CHAPTER XVII

FREDDIE FINDS A TRAIL

AT this moment, back at Meadowbrook Farm, everything was going well. Aunt Sarah and her helpers had just finished putting the apple butter into jars. "Thank you, Nan," her aunt said. "You've been a big help. Why don't you go outdoors now and play? I'll clean up."

"I'll look in at Harry's pigeons," Nan said. "Maybe they need attention."

As Nan walked across the yard, she could see Freddie and Flossie playing under one of the apple trees.

Nan climbed to the roof and peered into the loft. She noticed two pigeons strutting about the floor.

"They have something on their legs!" she thought in surprise. Nan opened the door and walked in. Then she picked up one of the birds to examine it. Quickly she pulled off the rubber band and unfolded the paper.

"How exciting!" she thought after reading Bert's note. She unfastened the capsule from the leg of the second pigeon and hurried down the steps.

"Freddie! Flossie!" she called when she got outside. The small twins came running.

"What's that in your hand?" Flossie asked.

Nan explained about the note which she had found on the pigeon's leg. "And here is the message Bert wants us to figure out."

The three walked to the house and settled themselves on the porch. Nan pulled the paper from the capsule.

"What does it say?" Freddie asked eagerly.

"Every girl raves about boys!" Nan read, a confused expression on her face.

"What does 'rave' mean?" Flossie asked curiously.

"Well," said Nan to her small sister, "it sort of means to be crazy about something."

"Oh," Flossie commented, thinking this over.

Freddie giggled. "Bert and Harry are teasing you!"

"Bert doesn't think it's a joke," Nan explained. "He thinks it might be a code message from the bank robbers!"

"I know what a code is!" Freddie practically screamed. "It's a secret message!"

Flossie looked puzzled. "You mean we're

not s'posed to be able to read what it says?"

"That's right," Nan agreed. "Sometimes when a person wants to send a secret message, he uses one word to stand for an absolutely different word so that a stranger reading it won't know the correct meaning."

All three studied the paper until Nan finally spoke up, "Maybe instead of 'every' the person who wrote this means some other five-letter word beginning with 'E.'"

"But how can you tell what he *does* mean?" Freddie insisted.

"Let's just see if we can figure it out," Nan said.

The three children worked for a long time without success. Then Aunt Sarah came out on the porch. "Dinner is ready," she said. "I wonder where Bert and Harry are."

Nan told her about Bert's note saying that they were going to the cabin.

Aunt Sarah looked worried. "We'll start dinner without them," she decided, "but if they're not here by the time we finish, I'll call the troopers. Your uncle has gone to town and won't be back until late this afternoon."

During the meal, everyone listened eagerly for the boys' return. When the last bites of apple dumpling had been eaten, Aunt Sarah stood up.

"It's almost two o'clock," she said. "I'm

afraid something has happened to those boys. I'll speak to Lieutenant Kent."

She went to the telephone, and shortly afterward the trooper arrived. Trooper Bennett was with him. They jumped from the police car and came up onto the porch.

"You've lost some boys?" Lieutenant Kent asked jovially. "Don't worry, we'll find them for you!"

"Where do you think they might have gone?" Trooper Bennett inquired.

Nan showed them Bert's message and told about the cabin in the woods.

"Do you think you could find your way there?" Lieutenant Kent asked her.

Nan nodded.

"Okay! Let's go!"

The three children got in the police car, and the trooper drove to the edge of the woods. Then with Nan in the lead, they began the trip through the wooded area.

After almost a half hour's walk, Freddie cried out, "I see it! There's the cabin!"

The police officers broke into a run, and the others followed excitedly. But when they reached the cabin, it was empty.

"The boys must be around here somewhere!" Nan burst out. "Bert *said* they were going to the cabin!"

"He's left us a trail!" Nan cried

"We'll take a look among the trees," Trooper Bennett said briskly, beginning to push aside bushes and underbrush.

Freddie saw a chipmunk and followed it among the trees. Suddenly the little animal stopped and began to nibble at a small pile of grain on the ground.

"That's funny!" Freddie thought. "It looks like pigeon feed, and there's some more of it up ahead!" He shooed the chipmunk away and called to the others.

When they came running, Freddie pointed to the seed. "Bert had a pocketful of pigeon feed last night," he said. "Maybe he dropped this."

"He's left us a trail!" Nan cried excitedly. "See, there's some more!"

"If it *is* a trail, Bert's a pretty clever boy," Trooper Bennett said admiringly.

The group walked slowly. At times the trail of seed disappeared entirely. Then one of the children would run ahead until another bit of grain was spotted.

They went on in this way for a long while, then Nan suddenly dashed forward. "I see them!" she cried.

The others ran after her. There were Bert and Harry tied to a tree Indian-fashion, back to back. Handkerchiefs had been stuffed into their mouths so they could not call out. Lieutenant

Kent pulled the gags from the boys' mouths
while Trooper Bennett cut the ropes which
bound them.

"Thanks!" Bert cried, rubbing his numbed
arms. "I guess you found my seed trail!"

"Yes, we did, Bert!" said Lieutenant Kent.
"You really used your head. Now tell us what
happened."

Bert and Harry told the troopers that they
had been seized as they walked along the forest
path looking for pigeons. Two men, one of them
very tall and thin, the other stockier, had tied
them to the tree and then run away.

"Didn't they say anything?" Nan asked.

"Yes," Bert replied. "While they were tying
us up, the thin man said, 'We have to get out of
here fast. We'll pick up the loot and meet the
boss tonight!' "

"What!" Lieutenant Kent exclaimed. "Those
men must belong to the gang of bank thieves."

Trooper Bennett said, "If we could only find
out where the loot is hidden!"

"Suppose we take these children home, then
we'll do some scouting through the woods," the
lieutenant suggested. "Come on, boys."

Aunt Sarah was relieved to have the two
back. "I don't want any of you children to go
into the woods again until those thieves are
caught!" she said firmly.

"Did you figure out the message?" Bert asked Nan eagerly when they all went out to the porch a little later.

"No," Nan said. "I just couldn't seem to get it. Let's try again now!"

The children got paper and pencils and gathered around a table.

"Maybe the first letter of each word forms the message," Bert suggested. He put them down. "They spell EGRAB."

"E grab! I grab!" Flossie chanted teasingly.

Bert looked discouraged. "That certainly doesn't mean anything," he admitted.

The children went through the message again and again, putting the five letters in different order.

Finally Nan looked up. "Bert! That first word you made—egrab—if you spell it backwards, it's barge. Could that be a clue?"

"Barge!" Bert exclaimed. "Of course—the canal barge!"

"The men are to meet the boss on the canal barge!" Harry cried.

At that minute Uncle Daniel drove up to the house. The children dashed to meet him as he stepped from the car.

"Well!" he said. "What's all the excitement about?"

Harry quickly told his father of the day's

events and the mysterious message which he and Bert had found on the strange pigeon.

His father was very interested. "I'll call Mr. Taylor and ask about the barge," he offered. "He's the man who owns it, and he'll know who's been on it."

The children stood by the telephone while Uncle Daniel talked to his friend. "I'm afraid you'll have to figure out something else," the farmer said when he had completed his conversation. "Mr. Taylor tells me that the barge is safely moored to the dock for the night and that no strangers have been around it."

Everyone continued to talk about their disappointment at not finding the meaning of the mysterious message.

After supper Bert said to Harry, "I still think the barge has something to do with that message. I'd like to look at it."

"So would I," Harry agreed. "I'll ask Dad if he'll take us down there."

When Uncle Daniel heard the request, he admitted that he was also interested in looking over the barge.

"Do you want to come, Nan?" Bert asked his twin.

"Of course," she replied.

Freddie and Flossie had been listening to the conversation. "We want to come too!" Freddie spoke up. "Don't we, Flossie!"

"All right," Uncle Daniel agreed, "but you must stay with me and not wander off."

The small twins gladly promised to behave and the group set off. It was dark by the time Uncle Daniel stopped his car along the road.

"This is as near as we can get to the canal," he said. "We'll have to walk from here on."

The children jumped from the car and followed Uncle Daniel across a dark field. It had been recently plowed and the walking was difficult. Several times Flossie stumbled and fell.

As they drew near the canal, Bert, who was in the lead, suddenly stopped. "Look!" he cried. "The barge has lights on it!"

Ahead, through the trees and bushes which grew along the edge of the canal, they could see the dim outline of the canal boat. A light glowed at one end of the barge and another light seemed to move back and forth on the deck.

"Someone's there!" Nan exclaimed.

"All right, let's try to get near enough to see what's going on," Uncle Daniel directed. "Stay behind me." He moved forward.

Suddenly a figure jumped from a clump of bushes in front of them. "Halt!" a voice rang out.

CHAPTER XVIII

AN EXCITING REWARD

AT THE sharp command Uncle Daniel and the children stopped short. "Who are you?" the farmer asked quickly.

"I own this property and that boat," the man replied gruffly. "You're trespassing. Get out!"

"Oh, no, you don't own it!" said Uncle Daniel. "We think you're helping the bank robbers."

With a lightning movement the farmer tackled the man, who collapsed on the ground with a loud grunt. When the man opened his mouth to yell, Uncle Daniel thrust a handkerchief between his teeth.

"Quick! We'll tie him up!" Uncle Daniel directed and pulled off his leather belt.

In a second he and the boys had the man's hands secured behind his back. Then Bert and Harry tied their prisoner's feet together with Bert's belt.

"We must get the police!" Uncle Daniel said as he rolled the helpless man under a bush.

"I'll get them!" Nan volunteered eagerly.

"All right," Uncle Daniel agreed. "There's a house on the other side of the road up a little ways. You can telephone headquarters from there."

"Freddie and I'll go with you, Nan," Flossie spoke up.

"That's a good idea!" Uncle Daniel approved. "The boys and I will keep watch on the barge until the police come."

Nan and the small twins sped off in the darkness. After they had gone, Bert turned to his uncle. "I think we should try to capture the men on the barge," he said worriedly. "I'm afraid they'll get away before the troopers can reach here!"

Bert outlined a scheme for holding them.

"We'll try it, but be very careful," his uncle warned.

He and the boys walked toward the barge. When they reached the edge of the dock, all of them stepped behind trees.

"Hello there!" Bert called out in a deep voice.

The beam of a flashlight pierced the darkness. It struck Uncle Daniel, who quickly turned his face away.

"We've got the loot," a man called from the barge. "Is everything ready?"

"A-OK," Bert called again. "Bring the stuff off."

A few minutes later two men stepped from the barge onto the dock. One was tall and thin, the other of medium height and stocky. Each carried a heavy sack over his shoulder.

"They're the ones who tied us up," Bert whispered to his uncle.

When the men reached the shore they paused. At that moment Uncle Daniel, Bert, and Harry jumped them. The tall, thin man dropped his sack and ran. But the stocky man was held tightly.

Suddenly Bert exclaimed, "Look!" The woods were dotted with little lights which moved swiftly toward them.

The next minute Lieutenant Kent ran up to the group. "Need some help?" he called out, pulling handcuffs from his pocket.

"The troopers!" Harry said thankfully.

"We're all here—police and FBI! Got a call that you had captured the bank robbers!"

"Quick!" Bert cried. "One of them got away!"

"A tall, thin fellow?" the trooper asked. "We got him when he ran up the road!"

"There's a third man under a bush back

"The troopers!" Harry said gratefully

there," Uncle Daniel told the trooper.

When the boys and Uncle Daniel reached the road, they found Nan and the small twins. They were watching the three handcuffed men being put into a patrol car.

Lieutenant Kent came up to the Bobbseys. "Those are the bank robbers all right," he said. "It looks as if all the money they got from the banks is in those sacks. We're taking them in to the Meadowbrook jail. If you want to talk to them, come in tomorrow."

As the Bobbseys drove toward the farm, Bert spoke up. "Those two men almost fooled everybody. They didn't go away. They doubled back here with more loot."

"I wonder," said Nan, "if they sent that message to their boss telling him they had hidden the money on the barge."

"And they never knew he didn't get the message," Harry added with a chuckle. "We found the pigeon, and Nan broke the code!"

"But how did they send the warning on Harry's racing pigeon?" Flossie wondered.

"I vote we go to the jail tomorrow and find out exactly what happened!" Bert proposed. "We don't know yet who the boss is."

"Yes! Yes!" the others chorused.

The children went to police headquarters the next morning. At once the officer in charge welcomed them warmly and congratulated them on trapping the prisoners.

"The men have confessed to the bank robberies," he said. "They made their headquarters in the woods, but when people came around, they hid on the barge. They didn't dare use the green car any more, and went off on foot at night. They rented cars, then left them in different places."

"I'd like to know how they used pigeons and where they kept them," Harry said.

"I'll let you talk to Slim. He seems to have been in charge of that. I want you to make a formal identification of him, anyhow."

The officer gave an order, and in a few minutes the tall, thin man was brought into the room. He eyed the children with disgust.

"I hate to think that all our good plans were spoiled by a bunch of kids!" he burst out.

"Did you really use carrier pigeons to send messages out of the woods?" Harry asked eagerly.

"Sure," the man replied. "You and that other boy almost found the cage we kept them in when we caught you in the woods yesterday!"

Lieutenant Kent had walked in and overheard the last remark. "Good morning," he said. "You will all be interested to know that the police found the pigeons. We let them loose one by one and followed them in a helicopter. They took us right to the boss of the bank thieves. He's now in jail."

The slim man hung his head. "I wish I'd never agreed to work for him," he said sadly.

"I have homing pigeons too," Harry spoke up. "One of yours hurt his wing and landed on our basket. We found your message!"

"So that was it!" The thin man moaned. "The boss never got our word! It must have been one of your pigeons who dropped in on mine one day. Of all things—I sent *you* a message that time. But it didn't do any good!"

Suddenly Bert had a thought. "What about the animals that disappeared from the Holden farm? Did you have anything to do with that?"

The man looked more cheerful. "That was one message that got through! We asked our pals to get those animals out of the way. They were bringing too many people near our hide-out!"

"It was a mean thing to do!" Nan spoke up indignantly. "But Arthur got away from you!"

"Who's Arthur?" the thief asked. "Our men weren't supposed to kidnap anyone!"

Freddie giggled. "Arthur's a bear! I guess he jumped off the truck and hurt his leg."

"But he's all right now," Flossie said with satisfaction.

The prisoner was led away. The children chattered excitedly all the way home. By the time they reached Meadowbrook Farm again, the Bobbseys felt content they had figured out the answers to their questions about the bank robbers.

"Let's ask all the camping crowd over this afternoon," Harry proposed. "They'll want to hear how the mystery was solved."

At three o'clock Bud and Tom came up the lane. In a few minutes Kim and Patty followed. Bert told the story of the capture.

"Oh, I think you're wonderful!" cried Kim.

"How did you ever have the nerve to do it?" Patty asked, and the Bobbseys laughed.

"You sure are good detectives," Tom Holden said admiringly after hearing the whole story. "I wish I could have found all those animals they let loose," he added wistfully. "My mother and dad are coming home next week, and they'll feel pretty bad about the missing bears."

"I'll catch you some bears, Tom!" Freddie promised seriously.

The children stopped talking as a car came up the lane. A tall, gray-haired man stepped out. Uncle Daniel met him and the two went into the house.

"It's Mr. Crane!" Harry explained. "He's the president of the Meadowbrook Bank."

A few minutes later Mr. Crane came from the house with Uncle Daniel and Aunt Sarah. They walked toward the group of children.

"Mr. Crane has something to tell Harry and the twins," Uncle Daniel said. "I thought you all might like to hear it."

"Is it a s'prise?" Flossie asked, running up to her uncle.

"I hope it will be a happy one," Mr. Crane said with a twinkle in his eyes. "Perhaps you have heard that the Meadowbrook Bank was offering five hundred dollars for the capture of the men who had robbed our bank." He paused.

"I heard it on the radio!" Tom said.

"Well, the bank board met this morning," Mr. Crane went on, "and decided it should be awarded to the five Bobbsey children who found the thieves!"

"Oh boy!" Freddie exclaimed. "Five hundred dollars!"

"That's a hundred for each of us," Harry pointed out. "What are you going to do with yours, Bert?"

His cousin looked uncertain. He glanced at the other twins.

"I know what I'd like to do with mine!" Nan said, her dark eyes dancing with excitement.

"What?"

"Will you wait a minute while I speak to the

other Bobbseys?" she asked. Nan pulled Harry and the twins away from the visitors.

The five children huddled together while Nan talked. Then Bert said, "Neat idea."

"Of course!" Harry agreed.

"It's a bee-yoo-ti-ful plan!" Flossie exclaimed.

"I'll tell Mr. Crane!" Freddie offered.

When they rejoined the others, he said with a broad grin on his face, "We're going to spend the money to buy more animals for the Holdens' Animal Farm!"

"Mostly bears!" Flossie added happily.

Tom looked overjoyed, and the rest clapped their hands.

Kim added, "We always have such a wonderful time when the Bobbsey twins come to visit Meadowbrook!"